P9-ECN-307

Mozart, Westmoreland, and Me

MOZART, WESTMORELAND, and ME

STORIES BY

Marilyn Krysl

NEW YORK

Published in the United States by

Thunder's Mouth Press, Box 780, New York, N.Y. 10025

Design by Loretta Li

Grateful acknowledgment is made to

the New York State Council on the Arts

and the National Endowment for the Arts

for financial assistance with the

publication of this work.

Some of these stories first appeared

in The John O'Hara Journal, Matrix,

The Mid-American Review, Triquarterly,

Guest Editor, Prism Magazine, *and* Telescope.

Library of Congress Cataloging in Publication Data

Krysl, Marilyn, 1942– Mozart, Westmoreland, and me.

I. Title.

PS3561.R88M65 1985 813'.54 85-8043

ISBN 0-938410-30-X

ISBN 0-938410-31-8 (pbk.)

Distributed by PERSEA BOOKS INC.

225 Lafayette, New York, N.Y. 10012, 212-431-5270

For my father who taught me Mozart

And my mother who gave me the wherewithal

The Artichoke

> . . . until we take into account his most personal views about the artichoke, the glove, the cookie, or the spool.
>
> BRETON, NADJA

It will happen on a train to Banff, both of us thinking we're on a vacation. We'll be in the dining car, smoking and discussing Baudelaire or discussing Gulf Oil or discussing inflation while we wait for the waiter. While we wait for the waiter, in no hurry, and not really very hungry. And in this discussion we'll use the expressions *GNP* and *market value* and *idea of evil*. And it will be you and I talking, not somebody else somewhere else, and not some fake couple got up for fiction.

The waiter comes to take our order. He's black, in a white jacket. He'll be black because that's how waiters on trains to Banff are; it's the decision of the railroad to conduct its business in this way. We'll wish he weren't our waiter, but there you are. And there we will be while the waiter waits as he's paid just enough but not too much to do, until I've made my point about Baudelaire and we break off this discussion to order.

The tablecloth will be starched white linen. Not because we want starched white linen, but because if you take a train to Banff you get a white linen tablecloth. And we're taking this train through these mountains. The mountains won't be there for us, of course, but they'll be there.

And we'll order an artichoke. Because we like them. We like them, and there they are on the menu.

We know we can change some things but not others, and we know which ones we can change, when you kick a rock you break your toe, and now we're hungry. By this time we've dispensed with the waiter's blackness, the starch in the linen, the mountainous mountains, we've adjusted our feelings about them to this fact. We're also bored with these feelings that insist on hanging around like tedious children who have nothing to do, but mostly we're hungry. And everyone of course gets hungry, we can gather together around this point as around a table. Right now I could easily dispense with high-toned moral phrases and sit down with the chairman of the board of Gulf, as long as each of us had an artichoke.

Here comes the waiter with a white platter. I see the artichoke's rows of spiked leaves, leaves shaped like feathers, and closer now rounded to a point like feathers, much closer, and are those feathers coming closer those are really feathers—and now my hunger backs all the way up from my belly into my mouth, a heart that wants to fly out and away—it's feathers, it's a feathered headdress, it's a head—and the waiter sets before me the purple head of Quetzalcoatl on a tray.

I want to say *No*, you've mixed up my order with someone else's, I'm not the one who asked for this, take it away. *But Madame*, he says, *you ordered it*. And I want to say "Don't call me Madame!" But there is Quetzalcoatl's head on my tray.

What we ordered isn't what we want; you'd think any fool could see that. We've always assumed our gentle intentions excuse our imperial way of life. But we still haven't got used to a waiter bringing Quetzalcoatl's head on a platter, whose head we'd forgotten we were supposed to ask for, having gone on this vacation through mountains forested rugged amazing though no longer virgin, leaving the kids in school studying how to manage the Corporation, whose managers we'd comfortably managed to forget we are.

Contents

❊

Mozart, Westmoreland, and Me

Mozart, Westmoreland, and Me

Atalanta Soleil, of *Soleil and Westmoreland*. My name is first for advertising purposes.

That's Mozart at the harpsichord.

Westmoreland, with T-square and staple gun. Earmuffs and an army surplus greatcoat.

Under my parka I'm wearing my floral print.

Outside the cold is solid. Mozart works with an afghan over his knees. Stalwart Mozart. He will endure almost any hardship in order to keep working.

Mozart is known for *Don Giovanni*.

Westmoreland is known for the Chase Manhattan Bank.

I am known for arcades, aviaries, arboretums, observatories, and arches: Round, Horseshoe, Lancet, Ogee, Trefoil, Basket Handle, Tudor.

Westmoreland's favorite materials are reinforced concrete, pig iron, and lead.

My favorite materials are silk and velvet.

There are some problems.

Westmoreland works with earplugs. He wants to keep his alternatives clear and simple. He wants to keep me happy. He wants to keep the Ho Chi Minh Trail closed.

Westmoreland also works with a button at his fingertips. This makes me nervous. I bite my fingernails. I am tightmouthed and thinlipped. I press my thighs tightly together. All this makes ribbons of my concentration.

The button makes Westmoreland nervous too. But at the same time it's reassuring. He figures if he gets too nervous he can always push the button.

I work with a bowl of oranges at my right hand, a fresh gardenia in a jam jar at my left, a bottle of cognac on the shelf above me, a yellow cat asleep by the fire, a Navajo corn dance rug on the wall behind me, and the continent of North America spread out at my feet. I want to keep my alternatives open. I want to keep Westmoreland relaxed. I want to make the Ho Chi Minh Trail a six-lane highway, but I don't tell Westmoreland this. I don't want to rattle him. I don't want to excite him in any way. In a man like Westmoreland nervous tension can be fatal.

I work with a black desk phone at my fingertips.

Mozart works with a muffler and gloves. The music's great but the piano keys are cold. Mozart isn't nervous. He's obsessed with music. Everything else is flat. Eating, drinking, and idle chitchat are flat. There is no great extracted emotion in these things. People engaged in these things are vulgar and vacuous. Mozart himself feels vulgar and vacuous when he's not writing, performing, or listening to music. He is always exhausted when he eats and he eats without a thought in his head. He doesn't like himself when he has to do things like eat and converse with others. He doesn't feel like Mozart at these times. He feels constrained. He feels bored. He feels impatient. He wants to get back to the harpsichord.

The Queen of the Night wears a shiny black breastplate and helmet. She bares her fangs. She is not just evil and let it go at that. She's raising an army to do evil. She has been banished to the kingdom of the night by Sarastro the King, her husband. Their daughter, Pamina, was the Queen's one consolation, and now Sarastro has kidnapped Pamina. The Queen sings furiously. She will have revenge.

I don't want revenge.

Revenge is dated and exhausting.

I want to go lightly about my business. My business is arcades, aviaries, arboretums, observatories, arches.

I believe arches will save us. The arch doesn't push down. The arch lifts up. The arch invites us to be expansive. The arch invites us to crescendo. The arch invites us to embrace and burst into flame.

My arches are first-rate, and I want to get on with them.

Afterward I want a double cheeseburger with everything on it.

Westmoreland wants the Israelis to buy F1 fighter jets. Westmoreland wants the volume turned down.

—Yes sir, Mozart says.

Mozart wants the volume up here, in fact fortissimo, but he agrees to turn it down. He doesn't want to offend Westmoreland. He wants to keep writing music. He wants to keep writing music in hopes that his reputation will take off once again. When he was four he was invited to visit Maria Theresa. He spent Christmas at the court of Louis XV at Versailles. Now he is 35 and his childhood genius no longer seems remarkable. Salzburg is provincial. The Viennese did not like *Don Giovanni*. The Viennese are a spoiled, fickle people. Vienna is a woman who refuses to wear a dress more than once. When Mozart was 14 Pope Clement XIV signed the breve conferring on Mozart the highest class of the Order of the Golden Spur. He may freely enter the papal chambers at any time but he is not invited to sit at table with the nobility of Salzburg.

Sometimes Mozart simply cannot believe this. He is 35. He is a genius. When he meets Count Oettingen-Wallerstein on the street, Mozart screams I'm Mozart! I'm a genius! I'm Europe's darling! Salzburg is my hometown! I'm your offspring! I'm freezing! Give me five gulden!

—Keep the noise down, Westmoreland snaps.

—Yes sir, Mozart says. He changes it to pianissimo. He'll do almost anything to be allowed to stay at the harpsichord. Music is the only thing he knows. It's the only thing that makes him feel he's living at the top of his capacity. He will agree to almost anything if he's allowed to go on with his music. He works with a blanket draped around his shoulders, and hopes for the best. Damn the public. One must keep working.

But can we afford to damn the public? The cold is solid. The Palestinians are anxious. The Israelis are eager.

The button waits at Westmoreland's right hand.

Pamina is pure, but she is not just pure and let it go at that. Such innocence in a twenty-eight-year-old woman I have never seen. She has led a sheltered life, never allowed to go to the movies. She falls for a picture of the prince. She has no idea what pleasures her tits are for and when she thinks the prince has deserted her all she can dream up to do is plunge a knife between them. She runs back and forth in the snow, dagger in hand. Her coat is thin, hopeless gray. She wants to make up her mind. She must kill herself. Or be rescued. Or freeze to death.

I don't want to kill myself. I like it here.

I don't want to be rescued. I have always done these things myself. I am known for rescue. My shingle reads AMAZING RESCUE HERE ANYTIME DAY OR NIGHT.

And I don't want to freeze to death. That's why I'm with Westmoreland. He needs my name. I need his money. We need each other's body heat. I will stay with Westmoreland until I can figure out another way to do it.

Mozart knows one way and one way only to do it.

With his father, Leopold, he has been touring Europe since he was four. During this entire time there has not been a single summer. Even sitting on Maria Theresa's lap he shivered. The ladies-in-waiting rubbed his tiny hand to get the circulation going.

Mozart performed for the Emperor. The Emperor said well, it was no great feat to play when one could see the keyboard. Leopold covered the keyboard. Mozart played brilliantly. This, too, the Emperor said, was nothing special since Mozart used all his fingers. But to play with a single finger. That would be a real feat. At once Mozart performed several pieces brilliantly in this manner. Mozart saw the Emperor blush.

Mozart understood he had brought the Emperor to his knees.

Mozart felt the distance between the one standing and the one prostrate. He understood he was different from the average emperor. He understood the Emperor didn't like it. He understood he would not be invited again.

Mozart suddenly felt very cold.

He went immediately and wrote a concerto, two minuets, a string quartet, and *Ascanio in Alba*. By the end of the first act he felt all right again. In the second act he actually began to perspire.

—No sir, said Westmoreland. I'm just like the average American. And he immediately went to Florida. He figured boot camp would prove it. He figured boot camp would keep him warm.

I suspected the worst, but I refused to admit it. I didn't want to think about it. So I went and ate a lot of Hershey bars with my friend Charlotte. First I bought Charlotte a Hershey bar. Then she bought me one. Then together we bought a box of them and went and sat on Charlotte's pink chenille bedspread beside Charlotte's pink organdy curtains. Together we ate the whole box.

We got very fat. We figured now for sure we were just like each other. People treated us identically. With pity. With contempt. This was enough for Charlotte. Charlotte was happy.

It was not enough for me. In fact I worried it was all wrong for me. I began to imagine that what was wrong with me was Charlotte. That if I could just get rid of Charlotte I would be thin again.

—The trouble with you, I said, is you're a fat slob. Then I went home. I locked myself in my room and sobbed. When I was done sobbing, I did not call Charlotte on the phone and ask her to go roller skating with me. I went to sleep for three days and three nights.

When I woke up my mother said why don't you go see *Singing in the Rain*. As long as I sat in the theater and the musical whanged away I was fine. When the reel ended, there I was, alone in the dark. What do I do now? I asked myself. Then it got to the point where halfway through the movie I'd remember that the movie would end. Then it got to the point where if I thought about going to the movies I already knew what I would feel like afterward. Then I went into the living room and poured myself a shot glass of my daddy's Scotch whisky. Then I poured another.

I figured I would drink my daddy's Scotch whisky until I could figure out another way to do it.

The more I drank the thinner I got. I got so thin Ron Abell asked me to go out with him. Bruce Graham asked me to go out with him. Jeff Vanderberg asked me to go out with him. Brian Ellickson asked me to go out with him. Brian and I drank a lot of rum and Coke in the back seat of his parents' Chevrolet convertible. Then I went and got very sick. He went and got very sick too. He threw up all over my corsage. I threw up all over his white dinner jacket. When I woke up I understood I was failing. I went to the teacher and said *Please may I do extra credit*.

Ron Abell went into the Army.

Jeff Vanderberg went into the Air Force.

Bruce Graham went into the Navy.

Brian Ellickson went into General Motors.

I went around the world looking for arches. I was desperate. I went under every arch I could find. Then I went to UCLA and sat down and drew the bridge that spans the Amazon at Manaus. I drew the Benares Aviary. I did the working drawings for the Mt. Palomar Observatory.

On the way to deliver the drawings I stopped at the morgue to identify the body of my friend Charlotte. Charlotte never did like the cold in Phoenix. When she could not be cold anymore she climbed into the oven.

I recognized her by her South Eugene High class ring and her three gold fillings.

I felt the distance between the one standing and the one prostrate.

I understood I held power absolutely.

I understood there was no one like me anywhere in all of history.

I was afraid I would not be invited again.

If I am invited again, I said to myself, I will go and I will be grateful and I will keep my mouth shut and refrain from complaint.

When I came out, there was Westmoreland in his black Lincoln Continental.

Westmoreland sees my slender waist.

Westmoreland sees my abundant tits.

Westmoreland sees my fantastic pair of legs.

He says We can give you two dollars an hour.

I get into the car. I consider myself lucky that anyone at all will hire me after what I have done.

I get into the car. I figure I will work for Westmoreland until I can figure out another way to do it.

I get into the car.

Now I am leading an active life here at the drawing board, keeping my mouth shut and refraining from complaint.

Westmoreland is getting together some remarks he wants to deliver to Golda Meir.

Mozart is scoring the Prince's first aria.

The Prince is buying anything solid with authority. He has all the necessary body parts but his brain is fluffier than cotton candy. If Sarastro says We need you in Selesia he'll go. He has never seen a dead body. He has never seen a fat girl. Someone else, a nurse probably, has always run through the dragons for him. He doesn't know about the championship playoffs. He's never learned to drive a car. And I'm afraid he doesn't know about handwork and I will have to show him.

First you rub their hands and feet to get the circulation going.

Then you massage them all over with warm eucalyptus oil. This takes a long time, but you do it steadily. You do it with complete confidence that it will work. You do it until they are glowing. Then you wrap them in a comforter and go to make the tea. You sit with them and make sure they drink the tea. You sit with them however long it takes. You may have to tell them their name and get them to repeat it after you. You may have to lie down beside them and hold them. At least until they fall asleep. When they wake up they're ready to go back into the cold. From then on they're all right. They become great mathematicians, architects, trapeze artists, or work for the Department of Agriculture. Whatever they decide to do they turn out well.

Mozart is known for turning out great arias for sopranos.

Westmoreland is known for his leather chaps. For his hearty handshake. His austerity program. His multinational corporation. His ICBM. His mistress. His other mistress. His refrigeration car. His rational approach.

I am known for my remarkably warm response to his rational approach. I keep hot tea, a fur muff, and a burning bush at my fingertips. I put on gloves. I turn up the heat. I draw a hot bath. I pour kerosene on the fire. I fly to Bermuda in my yellow terry-cloth robe and sleep on the beach with my alarm clock. I tan. I tan some more. At last I fuck Westmoreland on the couch thinking *body heat, body heat*. But it's no good. Afterward Westmoreland is still shivering.

Some people are hopeless.

Some people are in their orchards tending their peach trees.

Some are riding in their *sedia* in the daily *passeggio* along the *Strada Nova* accompanied by torchlight and the boom of cannon.

Some people are cold.

Some are freezing to death.

Mozart puts more charcoal on the fire. It's no use. This little bit of charcoal isn't going to heat Europe. When Mozart was three Leopold built a small harpsichord. On this harpsichord Mozart learned to play. Leopold taught Mozart harpsichord, clavier, violin, and cembalo. He arranged all of Mozart's tours and accompanied him. He helped Mozart blow his nose when he caught cold. He looked after Mozart's laundry. And in Italy when Mozart suddenly shot upward and outward it was Leopold who with needle and thread pieced out his underwear.

In the Sistine Chapel Mozart first heard Allegri's nine-part choral work *Miserere*. The papal chapel guarded this work jealously. Copies were forbidden. Mozart copied the whole from memory.

Now only Haydn still believes in Mozart and will say so in public.

Leopold has been dead for four years.

Sarastro the King has been without a woman since he threw the Queen out. He tries to stay above any emotion with violent consequences. He likes being king and he makes elaborate shows of gentleness and wise understanding. He loves to dispense justice. He loves to have the final say. He loves to chair the meetings of the brotherhood. He loves to say I know but I can't tell you now. He loves to say I'm doing this for your own good. He loves to say One must keep working.

He doesn't like to fuck. Though he did once. Now he and the Queen have this healthy, buxom, Nordic daughter. But when you are fucking your work doesn't get done. There's no opportunity to show benevolence. And Sarastro couldn't figure out in this situation what Justice was or how to dispense it and he had to take off his gloves and robe and then getting his pants off wasn't easy one foot got caught while he hopped lurching on the other just managing not to fall then she whispered something dirty it came right up crowing like a rooster and she laughed and said wait not yet and then he couldn't figure out what to do just lying there looking at it didn't seem dignified and he tried to remember if Mrs. Finch had talked about handwork but couldn't and the fact that the lady was not embarrassed and was watching him with interest was embarrassing so when she said lie down it was something to do and he did and she came right down on top of him and then poof he had no say at all in the matter and when he opened his eyes there she was sitting on top of him big as a horse and looking very pleased with herself and there was no way he could get up without saying get off me so he waited humiliated until she kissed his nose, slid off, and curled up for a snooze.

Some people are nervous and clumsy and decide never again.

Some people are scared to death and will sign anything.

Some people are furious and will murder anyone walking harmlessly to the First Episcopal Church pancake breakfast.

Some people are secure in the knowledge they know exactly what they're doing.

What I'm doing right now is I'm moving this embankment out of my way with this International Harvester bulldozer, Westmoreland tells himself. What I'm doing is I'm bringing my left flank around behind the enemy attack force. What I'm doing is I'm smashing this dumb Chink in the face again and again with the butt of this my Army M1 rifle. What I'm doing with the aid and goodwill of Congress is I'm straightening out the mess General Taylor left me.

What I'm doing is hiding and biding my time until I can figure out another way to do it. Knowing nothing was brief. Now I know everything and I know it all the time. But I pretend I don't know. I wear floral prints. I wear a lot of eye shadow. I wear contact lenses so my eyes will appear to be fantastic deep dumb blue rather than watery knowing gray. I wear sunglasses. I smile. At parties I drink ice water with an olive in it. I go skiing at Sun Valley just like everyone. Given all these concessions I figure I might be allowed to listen to opera on the radio and to draw arches after hours.

Westmoreland puts in his earplugs.

—Tone it down, he says, gooses me, and uses my phone to put through his call to Golda.

—Yes, sir, says Mozart. Mozart has no dignity. Mozart has no shame. He will do anything Westmoreland tells him if he can just finish this opera. He sits down at the harpsichord and goes into a trance. When he was 22 he met Aliosia Weber. Aliosia was 18. She was a fabulous soprano. Together with her family they traveled to the court of the Princess Naussau-Weilberg. The father, mother, two sisters, and three brothers liked Mozart immensely. They were all very gay. Mozart wrote in his diary

I am happy to tell
you that we are well.
Through the world we go
though our funds run low.
But we're cheerful and bold
and none of us has a cold.

The cold is solid. Some people walk right through it. The Moor is not a Moor at all. He's a sweaty Italian tenor who plays soccer. Licking his chops he decides he will have Pamina tonight. Even if Sarastro doesn't want him to, and the moon, if the moon doesn't like it, can go behind a cloud. He cavorts on all fours like a chimpanzee. He is gleeful over the general excitement of daily life. Over all the little unwrappings and nifty surprises every minute holds. You can tell just by looking that he's known about handwork since he was 15. And he sneaks off to the movies every chance he gets and buys the biggest popcorn. For this Sarastro gives him fifty lashes on three successive afternoons. The Moor has the good sense to desert and join the Queen. The Queen has the good sense to offer him Pamina, if he can kidnap Pamina from Sarastro.

When Leopold discovered Mozart's affair with Aliosia he was furious. He sent Mozart packing off to Paris. To his mother. To cool off. To cool way down.

You have to be very cold to keep working.

Revenge is dated and exhausting.

Cold is dated and exhausting.

Waiting for events to turn is dated and exhausting.

Saying yes sir is degrading.

Working for the general staff is so degrading that if I met myself coming I would cross to the other side of the street.

I'm sick and tired of holding out against Westmoreland. I'm tired of Westmoreland letting me know he figures it's only a matter of time. He figures I will soon forget Charlotte's gold fillings. He figures that's life and one must keep working and that I will still want to link up with somebody and become a whole person. He figures I won't want to die without grandchildren. He figures he's doing me a favor. He figures he's a solid if not brilliant dancer. He figures after all those musicals I aspire to a musical life.

Mozart, Aliosia says, you are an extraordinary person. You don't know how to be an ordinary person. You don't know how to act in concert. All you can do is act alone. At best write magnificent arias. At worst jump up from the piano and lean over tables and chairs, somersault, and meow like a cat. You experience your most private moments on the public stage. I must call off our engagement.

Mozart does not like this analysis. But he's not dumb. He is forced to admit it's correct. He decides he must make the best of things. He marries Aliosia's younger sister, also a soprano. The sister's name is Constanze. When little Karl is born he feels mild elation and curiosity. Then he wants to get back to the harpsichord.

I want to finish this arch. Then I want a double cheeseburger, salad, a glass of beer and chocolate cake, a good fuck, and then more cake. And I want Westmoreland not to push the button.

Westmoreland wants something to happen soon. This suspense is making him tense.

The heat is turned up.

The fire is crackling.

The kettle is boiling.

The electric blanket is turned to ten.

The yellow cat is asleep.

Westmoreland and I are wearing our parkas.

A knock at the door. Mozart answers it. A stranger, dressed in gray, enters. He commissions Mozart to write a requiem. He will not reveal who he represents. Mozart is tearful with gratitude. He has no twentieth-century caution. He prefers to trust absolutely so he can go on writing music.

He hurries down to the butcher shop and buys a small portion of liver sausage. His teeth are chattering. Even in the Munich blizzard on the way from the hotel to the opera house this never happened. When Mozart was four he sat on Bach's lap and together they played four-handed sonatas. He thinks he has not been warm since.

He hurries back to his flat and begins at once. He works until he falls asleep on the floor. He works in this desperate manner for several days. The grate is cold. There is no more charcoal. He wraps himself in blankets and keeps working. He is feverish. He writes to Constanze, who is at Baden taking the cure with little Karl. "I feel such longing for something I cannot name. . . ."

It takes Constanze three days to return from Baden. Mozart recognizes her but can't get out of bed. He begins to sing the Prince's aria. Then stops. A profound depression comes over him. He does not want to look at Constanze, who is sitting beside the bed. Constanze is a solid soprano but she does not have the range and color Aliosia had.

Mozart turns his face to the wall and dies.

The Queen is marching.

Pamina is waiting.

The Prince, at Sarastro's suggestion, is walking through fire.

Westmoreland is cracking his knuckles. Westmoreland is looking in my direction.

The Moor is eating popcorn.

I am eating popcorn.

Mozart strikes me as a complicated, desperate man.

Westmoreland strikes me as a simple, desperate man.

Sarastro strikes me as a pompous ass.

Pamina is a dumb blonde, and the Prince's solemn piety strikes me as ridiculous. I laugh and slap my knee. The Moor leans over and whispers in my ear. What a dope, he says. I laugh. He laughs and slaps his knee and spills popcorn in my lap. I laugh and slap his knee. He laughs and slaps my knee.

Then I slap his knee and leave my hand on his thigh.

Westmoreland is furious. So that's the kind of woman I am. He opens the door. He's going to leave me forever. The military-industrial complex is walking out on me. This is good-bye. He steps forward resolutely smack against the cold.

The cold is solid.

He feels in the corners and up and down the doorjamb. Not a chink. He pounds with his fists. Kicks, cursing. He picks up my marble bust of Antonio Gaudi and hurls it against the opening. The bust cracks into seven pieces of varying sizes.

Now Westmoreland is really furious. He rushes to his desk and pushes the button hard.

Nothing.

He lies on it.

Nothing.

The cold is solid.

The button is frozen.

Westmoreland screams remarks I can't repeat here. He has never before had to give in to a button.

He slumps down at my feet and weeps.

Westmoreland wants me to drive him home in his Lincoln Continental. Westmoreland wants me to make him a bacon, lettuce, and tomato sandwich. Westmoreland wants me to go with him to the movies. Westmoreland wants me to dress well on very little money. Westmoreland wants me to perform the tea ceremony when we go to visit de Gaulle. Westmoreland wants me to clean out the cat's box. Westmoreland wants me to wear black and have a fire burning and the kettle boiling and rub his hands and feet until the circulation comes back.

I don't need to be rescued, hoisted in a sedan chair, and carried triumphantly into the city. I can walk. I certainly don't want this parka. Or this thin, hopeless gray or this chick black or this virgin white or this harmless floral print. And I don't want these sunglasses or this glass of ice water. I don't want this smile. Or this shrill, nervous giggle. Or these manners. Or this dispassionate restraint.

I toss all these useless trappings in a heap.

—Westmoreland, I say, I could be content sitting at your right hand at dinner. And I could be content sitting up straight at your right hand at dinner. And I could be content to mix your drinks, scramble your eggs, press your pants, rub your back, suck your cock.

But I don't want to oil your gun and call your limousine to take you to the airport.

And I don't want to empty your bedpan and take out your glass eye at night.

I don't want to dress your chemical burns, check your plasma supply, screw on your hook, tighten the wing nuts on your brace, and wheel your chair to the edge of the cliff to show you the sunset.

I don't want to get your coffin from Dien Bien Phu.

I don't want to die with my face to the wall.

Neither do I want to spend much time weeping.

I want to be invited again.

But I won't agree to two dollars an hour.

I bend down and kiss Charlotte's silver urn of ashes as I did not kiss her face, eyes, mouth in life. I aspire to a musical life.

Westmoreland, I say, call the Salvation Army and tell them to come pick up this junk.

He looks a little bewildered. Him, a former four-star general in the U.S. Armed Forces. But I can't be bothered. I don't have time, now that the business is in my hands.

And go get a pick or something and start hacking away at this ice, I say.

Yessir, he says.

Nosir, I say, and on your way back pick up another bust of Gaudi. By the way, I say, we can pay you two dollars an hour.

I go to the mantel and I kiss Charlotte's silver urn of ashes as I did not kiss her face, eyes, mouth in life. I turn down the heat, take off the kettle, unplug the electric blanket, take off my parka, turn the opera way up, and sing along with the Queen. I am a passing good soprano when aroused.

The Queen turns to me, tears of rage in her eyes.

He's got Pamina! she says, the bastard.

Listen, I say, revenge is dated and exhausting. You don't want revenge. Why don't you take off those boots, get rid of that blacksnake whip. Take off that ridiculous helmet and this impossible breastplate. Now look in the mirror. See? Isn't that a lot better? Now why don't you come along with the Moor and me to the movies.

Are you serious? she says. I'm evil incarnate.

On the contrary, I say. Anyone who could make Sarastro come can't be all bad.

And now our furious singing has waked the yellow cat. She stretches and arches her back. Notice, I say to the Queen, the beauty of the arch, the graceful, sensuous curve of its soft upswing, how it invites us to crescendo and burst into flame. And now we have to hurry, that's the wicked Moor leaning on the horn of his Maserati. We'll put him in the middle, he can hold the popcorn.

So I seem to have figured out another way to do it. After the movie we'll dance the rest of the night to smoky jazz, arching our torsos this way and that, the three of us. We'll crescendo, embrace, burst into flame. And when the Queen and the Moor are finally snoring, I think I'll just step outside and have a look at the night sky, that greatest of all arches.

That's where I intend to build next.

Désirs

My father lights a cigarette and says, addressing my mother, "Now, about these checks, Carolyn." He looks at my mother. It's the way the doctor at the end of the day, having had enough of his patients' complaints, looks at his nurse: cover for me, cancel my appointments, agree, do not even suggest any other course of action. It's my father, at once commanding and crude, indulgent to a point, then blunt. Thus he maintains a certain wavering but vibrant intimacy with my mother. Frank looks, we know each other tell me the truth. Are you in love with him or is this a flirtation. Are you in trouble have you done something irreversible. We have lived together now for twenty years you are a handsome woman I make very good money. Speak.

Level is the word. My father and mother level with each other. The pact they've made is absolute. One of them could commit murder and they would sit down and talk straight. Together they would figure out what to do.

My mother says nothing. My mother, standing beside the diningroom table, the vase and scissors and tissue paper and the long stalks of iris spread out before her. She hesitates only for a moment. Then she straightens ever so slightly into her full height and continues, picks up the scissors and trims the stem she's holding at a ninety-degree angle. She waits for him to continue. She's ready.

I am upstairs in my room nursing the life of the mind. The floor register is open, I can hear his voice, I can imagine her face. I'm as tall as my mother now and I'll probably get taller, I haven't stopped growing. I got my mother's looks and my father's height. I got my mother's looks but her handsomeness is transformed in me, muted, the line of my jaw softer, my features almost quivering where hers are firm. She is classic, I come later. The Greeks pick her, I belong in the Flemish school, Rubens and Vermeer, Renoir, leaning into the Impressionists. You can pin her down—you can't pin me down.

I got my mother's looks but I have not yet decided what to do with them. I lie on the bed reading Whitman, waiting for my friend Alex. I have already read Schopenhauer, Nietzsche and some Wittgenstein. Whitman is cake, a change. Whitman is the long grass after the steel expansion bridge. I am walking through this grass toward Chekhov, Tolstoi, Dostoevski.

And I will soon see Alex, she's on her way over. Alex of the trim Levis, the slim ankles, her firm breasts beginning to fill out. Alex, dashing in riding boots, long black hair tucked up under her cap. She has class, my Alex. She doesn't habitually smoke but enjoys now and then a Gauloise. Doesn't drink, except when I come and her parents give us Dubonnet with a lemon slice. She is not in the grip of anything; she stays serenely out of reach of the undertow. Like the good rider she is she sits lightly, easily in the saddle, she goes with the animal rather than rides it.

When Alex comes I will tell her about Whitman, how he unrolls the country before us, how huge it is, how much room there is in him, how vast and grand the space, how there is no end to the grass.

My father is handsome. It's gone a long way for him and still goes. He has sex appeal, my father; he's attractive to women. He has charm. A certain knowledge of himself is visible in his face. He knows what he likes and he knows his limits, knows what he can and what he can't do. But he *can* do a lot. Good body, good face, and basic sanity. I have to admire my father; he has managed to maintain a very pragmatic sanity. In the face of my grandfather's alcoholism, in the face of my grandmother running her world like many-armed Kali, Coatlicue with her skirt of snakes. My grandmother is Ta-Urt, hippo and crocodile, lioness and woman in one. "Ed," I have heard her address my father in his adulthood, "if you embarrass me I shall see to it that you suffer in turn."

He learned from her, my father did, took his view of the world from her. And he adopted her tactics but gave them his particular masculine style. He adopted her tactics but learned to play down their visibility, to temper his speech and tone. He has presence, he doesn't have to shout. My grandmother always says what she thinks; my father thinks what she thinks but generally keeps these thoughts to himself. He has kept and will probably keep this tempered sanity to the end.

And he's kept it, too, in the face of desire. He managed to channel his desires into the right places. Into the places my grandmother approved. He desired the right friends, the right contacts, the right kind of girls. He was careful. He still is.

Also my father became the object of my mother's falling in love.

You don't need to know where beautiful women come from. People don't want to know. They have no history, in fact history would be a liability. Only in novels do you find out about a beautiful woman's history, and you alone know, none of the characters in the novel know. People like the idea that this kind of woman is a miracle, making her sudden startling appearance on the scene. People like here and there a miracle. If a woman like my mother can keep her history hidden she can have any man she wants.

I imagine my mother walking into a crowded room, looking over the crowd, accepting a drink from the tray offered by the black waiter. Her eyes scanned the crowd, looking for something. Then she saw my father. Who had already noticed her, who had seen her come in. Who had seen her and tried to continue the conversation, to keep his mind on what the other man was saying. She watched until she caught his eye. He excused himself and came toward her.

It was that simple, that compelling. Now my father smokes and exhales, taps the ash with his index finger.

"Not the check for the coat," he says. "You look terrific in it. You know I wanted you to have that coat."

Neither facing him nor turning her back my mother places the iris in the vase. She is intent on these flowers and herself in relation to these flowers, the precise arrangement, the final effect. Though she lets him know by the way she stands that she's listening, he has her attention.

On my dressing table one white rosebud is beginning to open. I picked it, broke it off in the garden when I came in from school, and now in the warm water it's beginning to unfold. My head is full of Whitman's lush description of America, and I watch the rose opening, thinking about Alex, imagining her stride, the solid click of her boots on the pavement. I feel good remembering her quick smile when she sees me, the glint, the excitement in her eyes when she sees me.

My grandmother would admire Alex's classy style. My grandmother and Alex would look at each other and know immediately what not to say, how much distance to keep. I have told Alex about my grandmother, and she nods as though she already understands, as though she can easily imagine this woman. A woman she herself could become but has chosen not to become. They would look at each other, exchange a look of recognition. They would recognize face to face another version of their own resolve. Alex knows what she wants and has already decided to have it. My grandmother knew what she wanted but decided finally against it.

He has put out his cigarette and now he looks at her, waiting. He still loves to look at her, this has not diminished. *This woman is my wife,* he thinks as he watches her. And it seems to him on the one hand natural, but at the same time this fact still amazes him. That she actually is, has been for twenty years, his wife. This extraordinary woman, this striking woman, this compelling creature, this beauty in the gray and brown world. He loves her for her color and for the smoothness of her skin and for her laugh. He loves her for all the companionship he had been taught to live without. But did not want to live without.

And this makes him nervous. Because what he wants is my mother. What he does not want my mother to do is leave him. This is just about the only thing that makes him nervous. With my mother he took the biggest chance he will ever take.

When my mother walks into a room it becomes a different room. So different in fact that the Prince of Oman proposed to her in a room she herself had transformed. But by then she was used to this, the effect she had on people and places no longer surprised her. She knew she could have whatever she wanted, but she didn't want the prince. Because she had already met my father and she had decided that what she wanted was my father. The wealth of another being, of a personality and a soul that moves you—that excitement is far more interesting than any other kind of wealth. That was what my mother thought, and my father. They agreed on this immediately, they rushed together, they fell toward each other.

Although to be honest—and this must be obvious—my mother would never have married for love alone if the man she loved had had no resources. She walked into those particular rooms because she knew exactly how much money she needed. And she knew these were the rooms where men with that kind of money would be.

She didn't go anywhere it didn't pay to go.

And then, when she knew she was in the right place, she said to herself, *now, from among these*.

It should have been simple then, after they fell in love. You would think it would have been simple. Maybe the trouble is that my mother is a little too beautiful and has never been able to forget it. She knows too well her beauty is powerful but that it is the only real power she has. She knows my father needs her. She knows how far she can go and she goes only that far. And the other trouble is that my father is a little too much given to command. His sense of dignity, even of his sanity, depends on staying in command.

So that neither of them can let go, relax beyond a certain point. Beyond a certain point both of them have to keep somnething back.

"Carolyn," my father says now. He is about to make his speech, his proposition, to say his ultimate say.

I look away from Whitman's long flowing lines. The rose goes on opening, but I have begun to feel uneasy, to feel restless. My parents' voices sound very far below me, slightly unreal, like the voices of stick people, nothing to do with me. And yet they do, they have everything to do with me, and something in their voices urges me to do something, to move. Whitman's grassy plain is too smooth, the grasses' heavily seeded heads swaying invite you to lie down and sleep. And I must not sleep now, I must go on, I must get to where Alex is waiting for me, I must get through Whitman and on, on to Chekhov, Tolstoi, Dostoevski.

In the hallway outside my room hangs Sargent's *Désirs*. I imagine Alex walking through the stableyard, through the mud to the stalls where the horses are housed. Sun sweeps in at a low slant, and she takes the brushes and combs down from the shelf and begins to curry the horses, brushing the withers, loins, flanks of the horses, checking the fittings on the bridles, polishing the silver on the saddles. Testing the tautness of the strands of the girth.

The only sound now is the tinkling of silver fittings, the slap of leather against leather, the sound of the brush.

Now my mother turns to face him squarely. She is beautiful, she still is, and she is careful. She takes care of herself, spot-exercising every day, swimming laps three times a week, and she watches what she eats; she makes sure she eats well, calculates protein in grams, drinks rarely and very little. And she rests, she has managed to arrange for herself an active life laced with leisure, a life without much stress. A few tiny lines have begun to appear on her face, but they are infinitesimal. Still she is always aware—the knowledge like an antique trunk far back in her mind—that in ten, fifteen years her looks will go.

It won't be the same, she knows, for him. At age forty-five, sixty, and even later he will still look much like he does now. A few lines, a pound or two, possibly less hair. Though in fact it's even possible he will keep that thick shock of hair to the end, there is up to now no sign of its going. Well into his sixties he will be attractive to, will attract women, younger and younger women.

Nevertheless she knows she is central to him, absolutely central. Though this isn't because of anything she has done. It is rather because of who and what she is. The power of her beauty for him is a fact about him, not about her. She has done nothing but be.

And he knows, too, admits to himself how ineluctable is the fact of her centralness for him. And he knows she knows this about him. So it's not as though he could be surprised. But now he thinks he will play his next to last card; in fact he feels an irresistible compulsion to do this, he cannot resist.

"Carolyn," he says, "I want to give you something."

It will be something big. A month in Florence, Venice, Rome, Christmas in Lima, Christmas in São Paulo. Something big enough to stop the checks, big enough to placate my mother, big enough to leave my mother's dignity intact.

Far, far below me I imagine her turning to face him—and a chill, sudden and complete, comes over me. A chill, without warning, and I push hard against it—I do not want this ice across my skin! I sit up and reach for my hairbrush, listening. There is a pause, and I listen intently to this moment of peace—and let the brush drop into my lap: because at any moment now she will answer him, she will speak. *There is nothing I can do to stop them.*

They can't be stopped. They can't be changed either. They are who they are. And the time is coming and the time is coming soon, and I had stupidly imagined there was infinite time. This is an illusion books suggest, a glass of Dubonnet can give you this illusion. And there is the suggestion, too, of many possible courses of action, many choices, all equally possible. Only in the mind though can you have these illusions. Now my mother is about to speak, and for the first time I understand there are two choices and two only. I have held off this moment, pushed it back and back, and now the moment almost bursting is nearly here.

I will have to choose one way and choose soon.

"Ed," my mother says. She is holding an iris as she turns to face him. So that even before she speaks it will remind him, this stem burst into gorgeousness, precisely who this woman is.

This woman who is not me. Because I am neither my grandmother nor my mother. My face in this mirror is not Sumerian, not one the Greeks would especially admire. It's beautiful but the lines are too soft, blurred. And my frankness is too like a Renoir, and my strangely foreign willfulness, my desire to find my own way, is not the Greek way. I look at my face and it is already what it will become: one of the Dutch girls in the muddy stableyard stripping off their blouses, shoulders clear as lilies and ruddy, walking out into and over these grasses toward the pond where Monet's water lilies bloom, where Tolstoi's boat floats, waiting.

I do not want to hear it, what she will finally say. I cannot bear to hear it. And yet these people live and speak and I will have to hear her, I will have to know. There is no way to pretend they are not here, pretend they are not who they are. I know already by the way she stands, by the way she says his name, that what she is about to say will be cold and sharp, glinting and deadly as the scissors in her hand.

I do not want to witness these murders. But murder exists. I can't go on pretending the world is Whitman and Whitman only, I will have to move on. And in this world I, too, will need some metal. Not my grandmother's iron, not my mother's steel. But the supple, softer metal, maybe silver, of someone like Alex. Alex, Alex. It's she who can save me, she who can teach me to ride this like she does, she who will give me the secret of balance, the secret my grandmother and mother had to do without.

The girth is tight, the silver on the saddle gleams. The reins hooked over the pommel hold the horse's head back. And there is the bell, the bell—and I'm ready, I'm ready. In quick, short flicks I brush out my hair, as though I must get ready fast, as though I must look my best and quickly. And I take my cape from its hook, the rose from the vase.

"Ed," my mother says again, "listen." But I will listen no more, I leave my room without looking back. In the hallway I pass *Désirs—that way,* I say to myself. And I go downstairs, past the diningroom, closing my ears against the clipped cruelty of her voice. I don't look in. I don't want to see his face, her mouth. I go on down the hallway, down the last short flight of steps to the door.

And I open the door: here she is, Alex. Jaunty in her boots and cap, arms akimbo and smiling mischievously. She will keep to the end this cheeriness with its underlay of muscle.

"They're at it," I tell her, "at it again and finally."

She nods. She knows.

"And you're ready," she says, seeing my determination. She understands I have finally crossed the bridge, the grass. That I'm prepared to ride. That I'm ready for Tolstoi, Dostoevski.

"Yes," I say, laughing, and I hold out the rose. She takes it, laughing, and we stand there both of us laughing, looking at each other, this looking a glitter in our eyes. We are filled, filled with the bright energy of beginning, and this laughter of ours runs over, spills out of us and around us like the rippling of water.

"We'll just see," Alex says. "We won't make a map."

I nod. "I've got the books," I say.

"And the paintings?"

"I know where they are."

"Good," she says. "So come on," she adds, laughing again.

Around us the dark is purple, the stars like the eyes of mares. And the air is soft on my skin. There will be no abrasion. I swing the cape across both our shoulders then, and together we go down the steps laughing, we go down.

And Judith, Daughter of Ester, Raised the Sword Above Her Head

Give up the present.

They had it back there before 1944 for a while in Nebraska, but that's over. Oh they do beat the drum, selling this hot item, with hints on how to get the most from it. Be in the Now with Bodyworks. How to Flirt. Cliff Hanging for Beginners. As though the present still exists.

The future's all there is.

I didn't vote for the future, I never wanted microfiche. Liked holding a book in my hands. Liked the sun the way it was, took off all my clothes, gave myself to the sun hooklinesinker. The present was okay with me; I recognized myself. Looked in the mirror, and there was someone there! Hi! Hated my enemies and liked my friends well enough. I had my man, my little kid, all my teeth, and both my ovaries. I had my hair, my tits, and all my insides. Happy indeed, without hysterectomy, mastectomy, clitoridectomy, vericosurgery.

Even had a job that existed, deductions and all, ran the museum's information booth. Modest money, but I enjoyed the work.

Watched the lookers come and go, helped lost kids find their moms. Pointed professors toward Special Collections. Looked myself, listened to the guides.

"*Judith and Her Maidservant*," the guide would say, "dates from Gentileschi's Roman Period. It's and old-fashioned device to use a candle flame as the only light source, but notice how Gentileschi avoids the usual cliché effects. You can see how the darkness around the figures, deep and resonant, emphasizes the spirituality rather than the violence of the subject matter."

And so on.

The people looked hard. Studied the pictures. Little kids hung on to Mom's finger. Babes slept in arms. Silence pretty much prevailed, a few whispers. And nobody smoked; it was against the rules because of fire. They looked everywhere on the picture, lifted their little kids up to see. Me, too, every day I looked again, they were the same pictures but every day you looked at them differently. Life was full of little surprises, there were a good many moments of thrill.

Then they came to the exit, went out and somewhere drank a glass of wine, fed the kids chips. Watched the squirrels at play, talked. Nothing much happened, but it happened more excitedly.

I took a bus home, thinking about the pictures. Going over certain ones in my mind. A little music on the ride home, that's how my thoughts felt. Inside me was a healthy glow. The pictures came away with you, friendly.

At home my little kid looked good to me, not a brat at all. A fiesty light in her eyes, she was already on her way to becoming a maker of skyscrapers or a hotshot player of the cello. I couldn't wait for things to go on and on. And the evening sky had its sunset.

I spent a lot of quiet evenings in the present contemplating the general satisfactoriness of certain sunsets.

Then my man would come, we'd be busy for a while.

It was a modest life.

Now that's the future out there. Gray, they used to call it, now some fancy name or other, Smoked Petunia.

I'd have been happy hugging my faulty uterus to the end. But in the future they don't let you. Ovaries, too, and clipped my clit at the same time, cost-effective, save me money, they said. Make life simpler.

It did.

About the same time my man got it in the groin too.

—We need you! they told him. Special project, top secret, you'll be doing humanity a great service.

—No thanks, he said.

—Well, there's a little something in it for you.

He was tempted.

—Don't, I said.

So when they called him in he said, Thanks again, but I'd better not.

—Word's just come down, they told him, that this one is quick. Only a week, and a sizable sum for you and yours. And think of the contribution you'll be making. National honor. Hemispheric pride. President will host a banquet, more than likely.

Up went the flags, out came the bugles.

—Okay, he said, and signed.

Then the bugle playing taps.

Well I still had my little kid, now grown nearly all the way up. *Look at these swell dandelions* changed into *please I want panty hose*. And my job. So things went along for a while. Same pictures, same sunsets. Satisfactory enough.

Then it came time to kiss my tits good-bye. The doctor told me if I kept them I surely would die.

—Well I don't mind, I said. It's getting on near the time anyway.

—Nonsense, he said. A woman like you, a full life ahead.

—Behind, I said.

—Nonsense, he said. No reason you can't keep right on at the job.

—Still I'd like to keep them, ragged as they are, I said.

—But they're certain death, he said, and I can't permit that.

I've taken an oath, you see.

And he showed me the plaque to prove it.

So they went.

I didn't ask where, I didn't look down.

Then, gradually so you'd hardly notice, but nevertheless, the museum closed. People stopped coming, down to a trickle. Same thing all across the land; they lost interest. In the end the higher-ups decided to flood it, put in an ice rink.

It's an ice rink now, if you care for cold.

Just before they closed, then, I took off with one of the pictures. Not that anyone seemed to care. Carried it right onto the bus wrapped in the *Daily News*. A young one, not knowing, nearly put his foot through, I pulled it sideways just in time.

Hung it in my bedroom, nobody but me and my little kid goes in there.

So I had something. And hurt nobody, nobody wants pictures now. In the future they like shiny for the walls, and then what they do is sit at the viewscreens. Everywhere they got the viewscreens. The people real still like the old hypnotist got them. They don't even fidget. And you don't dare say a word or they're furious; they don't want anything but to stay there.

Nobody sitting at the viewscreens loves anybody else sitting at the viewscreens. It's *give me a cigarette, will you*. Also purists, they don't want anything, but they're like everybody else—ready: it's just the opportunity hasn't come. Back in the present there were opportunities. No one has seen one now for a while.

Minds go fuzzy, one leg goes to sleep. Who can remember their multiplication tables now? No one has seen an elephant lately. Sex is an empty suitcase, why eat a croissant.

Then the worst. I'd taken all of it, good-bye to my left kidney, so long to my hair. But this: my little kid grew up and then one day she got it. She got it and then blanked out. Found her standing on the sidewalk in front, like somebody just dropped her there. Her eyes whacko and the blood coming down between her legs.

Now she sits like them in front of the screens, except we don't have one. It's just a wall. Just sits, holding the edge of her blanket. When I come in and touch her shoulder she looks up, wonders who I can be. Her woman's face all wiped out. *Please I want panty hose* is gone, and her voice went, too, along with everything.

I take her by the hand to bed.

Then I'm alone.

So I sit in front of the picture. *Judith and Her Maidservant*, the little brass plate says.

Holofernes lies outside the picture. On the table you can see the edge of his armplate, dropped there in fatigue. He'd put in a day, and then some. A little pleasantness with Judith afterward. They left the candle burning. Then he began to snore.

The light from that candle shines like the sun, up all of a sudden at midnight. The sun, stunned up at midnight, by the startle of the deed.

The sword in Judith's hand, pulled back now, away from the light, is black.

Everything else white, in this light. This light on the robe of the lady Judith, holding up one hand to warn for quiet. On her hand, too, white like a beacon. On the turban of her maid, crouching, looking up. And on the maid's helpful, willing face. They look at what they have done, satisfied he will be still now. The heat of their deed still in them: you see it plain, making them both huge.

How big and white they are, these two! Judith's arms and the arms of the maid more like the shoulders of horses. Their arms and shoulders gorgeous, and huge with light.

Even then they knew what was coming. And did the best they could at the time.

His head at the maid's feet, shadowy. She's wrapped it up to carry back to camp.

So I sit and look and look my fill. That lady could paint, Gentileschi. I sit and look, and look my fill, and sometimes I say her name over to myself. Gentileschi, I whisper. Gentileschi. Lady, thy deed be done.

Macroscopic Phenomena

. . . the basic unit of the
universe is an event. . . .
—ZUKAV

Brian. He is not attractive at twenty-two, he wasn't attractive as a kid either. Even as a baby he acted limp, puked excessively, and lay around in smelly lethargy as though he hadn't the heart for living. Worried his mother into specialists and Valium (though she had other reasons, too, for the Valium). His life has not been anywhere near bliss. Father a famous research physicist and prestigious university professor, upstanding in the international scientific community. Mother now fat and frumpy, excessively even-tempered, she makes the average citizen of Palo Alto want to scream. She will go through life as she is now, a doily in the computer age. The father sublimates.

This father, this mother: Brian becomes a brain. Thrust into Advanced Calculus at an early age by the name they conspired together to give him: Brian. He is fat and soft. He is ill-shaped. All grace, beauty, stylishness, and verve have slunk inside, impacted in the cortex. Thick-lensed bifocals, honor roll, Merit scholar, he is destined late in life to receive a Nobel Prize. Indeed there will be no escaping such a prize. You think Destiny doesn't exist, we are self-made women and men? This kid is so destined your heart aches. In Rilke's terms he will fail utterly. He will not be able to change his life.

Beth talks intelligently incessantly. It's her method of not thinking too deeply about things she can't do anything about anyway. Majoring in economics. She is smart and a workhorse. Okay looking, a brunette, and completely willing to marry Brian. She has already been looking around, and he is what she can aspire to. Beth promises no surprises, none. It does not even occur to her to feel desperate about her prospects. That mild inner hysteria seems denied her, or she herself denies herself such little flurries of scariness. Will Beth turn fat and even-tempered in his arms? Or does she have inner resources not immediately apparent? Or the years, going by, may force her to develop resources. The intriguing thing is that if she decided to have style, she'd become a compelling figure. At present though she appears to be eager to nail Brian, this man so unattractive no coed will be persuaded into his sack no matter how prestigious the linen. She is at Stanford, he is at Stanford, last semester of the B.A., then graduate school and the tedious plodding ahead. He has no women: he has friends. Correction: he has, if he wants her, Beth. Anyway, he can marry her and presto, he'll be set, will get to have sex at last. Do not sniff at this, you who have health, joyousness, shapely torsos, and undistinguished parents.

The friends. A crowd of other brains, high school class presidents, some foreign students, mostly men. I like André, mother a French princess, father a Hungarian businessman. He treats Beth with respect, with Laura he's affectionately playful. Every now and then he winks at her and says, "I am lookeeng out for your velfare, darling."

Raoul, Sekiko, Franz. And Manuelo, who fled Spain to avoid Franco's draft. Managed to marry an American high school girl, though the marriage was never consummated. She has conveniently disappeared (who knows where—one believes only some of what Manuelo says), leaving him with American citizenship as long as she doesn't sue for divorce.

A few women like Laura and Beth. Beth tolerated more or less for Brian's sake, though he cannot get up the energy to want her. André and Manuelo try to rig various setups for him, they even contract with a young coed to pretend to fall in love with him. She's convincing, but at the vital moment he's too terrified to get it up. She shrugs and dresses, leaves rather abruptly, he thinks. When she tells André what happened, he has no choice. Matter-of-factly he sighs and pays her. Now these friends have given up. Brian will have to remain a virgin until he marries, there is nothing more they feel they can do.

Laura. Attractive. At first glance your American girl-next-door, athletic, shapely—but with flair! She has style the girl-next-door doesn't. "You are not," André says, "zee average greengo, darling." Great legs, she walks like an antelope. Slings one thigh across the other knee, calf swinging, swinging, as she takes notes. In Aesthetics 495 André whispers, "Watch out, darling, theese eediot beehind you is sneeking looks at your legs." Undistinguished, workingclass parents, no help to her, possibly a hindrance. (Act as though you have sprung from the head of Zeus.) There is no history of success, the absence of success is, in fact, a spectacular absence. The problem of sociology taking over personality: son of prof learns to become prof, daughter of housewife learns to stack a dishwasher. There is no escaping history, the trick is to make it work for you. In other circumstances, a moneyed family say, she might have become a Claire Booth Luce. But she has no capital, none, she's on a scholarship. What she has is style and quickness. She's going places, emphasis on the going. Blazing into the future here at Stanford, citadel of knowledge. Inside a university there is supposed to be immunity, as in a cathedral. To the extent this immunity exists she takes advantage of it. She may become an intellectual, perhaps another Simone de Beauvoir. Possibly there will be a grand passion, the love story of the century, possibly she will move from one painter, writer, sculptor to another. Or cast men aside and become a crack journalist, or make it at the U.N.; her French is fast becoming impeccable. She is talented at languages, digs philosophy, and she has been around, knows the nether workings of the body. A lawyer, a Nepalese student, a high school principal, the editor of the *Palo Alto Star*, briefly. Professor J, who fell in love with her and proposed (she refused). Laura believes in love, she has to believe in love. Laura has inherited nothing but bootstraps, and she isn't buying that line for a minute. As every public school pupil knows, Lincoln is a myth created by the U.S. Textbook Commission. God does not help those who help themselves, she will have to make it on her looks and brains. But this is a weighty prescription: everything is on the line all the time. Laura sometimes envies Beth the ease with which she assumes the world was created for her. On the outside Laura looks lush, but inside she's prepared a torso of steel. And steel adds weight—there has to be something with wings, something feathery on which to soar. A belief in love is the ticket. Like helium, it will lift her off. The fifties are finished and the sixties haven't quite got going, one of those moments in history when everything seems possible. She spent the fifties growing up, now here she is: like Cyd Charisse she's ready to dance.

Scene I

Laura and Manuelo were drinking espresso. André, in his room, read Wittgenstein.

"This think you call love, it's an illusion," Manuelo said, smoking one of André's Gauloises. (André had taken him in hand. "You vant to look like a man, you must shave," André instructed. "Every day shave. Vonce a veek, eetes not eenough for you.") "Sex is real," Manuelo continued. "All the rest, that's in your head." She laughed. Manuelo, lucky to get one girl in six months, maybe he'd never actually had one. Laura could afford to be gracious, let him have, for a while, her exquisite attention. Now that she'd laughed, though, he was annoyed. "You're too young to understand these things," he said. He was younger than she was but pretended otherwise.

"Look, Manuelo," she said, turning serious, "you can pretend it doesn't exist. But you're pretending."

"Illusion," he repeated firmly. "You're going to cry tears over this, sweetheart, believe me."

"I probably will, and precisely because it isn't an illusion."

"Listen sweetheart," he said, leaning across the table, garlic on his breath, "let Manuelo show you once. Some real sex and you won't want these dreams."

She fell back against the pillows, really laughing this time.

"Let's go to my room," he persisted. "We'll have some wine."

"André!" she called giggling. "Help! André!" André appeared in the doorway, took off his glasses.

"Vat's going on? Manuelo, I told you, she doesn't *vant* you. Quiet please, I beg you."

It's been raining lightly for several days, a wet spring, the azaleas are out fabulously. Kennedy in office for three and a half months, he looks like a winner, he just may be the one. Laura, just coming from a tryst with the lawyer, she's hungry. Of course she isn't in love with him, but while she waits he passes the time. A bit acrobatic, but it will do, interim. Laura doesn't think of a man as a catch; "a good match" doesn't interest her. Her scanner isn't tuned for the neutron star, her scanner is tuned for colliding galaxies. Now she is hungry and her skin glows. Beneath a yellow umbrella she walks quickly toward the Student Union, imagining the grilled cheese sandwich she will order, the glass of milk, the cherry pie. She would like a platter of tomatoes niçoise, but the grill doesn't serve such things, she'll have the tomatoes at home, later. Though Laura and Brian share some of the same friends, they have never actually had a conversation. They've been at the same table with André and the others, conversations everyone around the table plays into, as though conversation is a striped beachball—if it comes in your direction, give it a push. When they've met, it's been in these circumstances. For Brian's part, you don't take seriously what you can't have. She glances at him casually, he does not hold her eye. Now because of her umbrella she doesn't see Brian. But he sees her. He looks at her, and his guard is down—sweet circumstance that sometimes comes to us. Suddenly he's enjoying himself immensely: watching her when she is unaware of him, outside her window in the dark, looking in. The secrecy of this! People unaware of being watched are naked. She is striking in dishevelment, wisps of hair astray, and in her urgency, the decision in her stride. He can even see the tryst she still smells of, and how very hungry she is. He steps out to rush after her, take her to lunch—and stops: what in God's name has got into him, the impossibility of such rash action! He thinks to retract the energy of his longing—longing that soars from him in an arc—but in spite of the years of rigorous training, he isn't hardened enough to manhandle his response. Besides, his intelligence is uppermost, he knows a good thing when he sees one. He tries, in that split-second, to keep his feeling a twinge only, but he's leaned in just a little too close.

The Strong Force binding the nucleus together zaps him in.

The ache of love comes on like instant acne. Unlike a pimple though his feeling has a graceful shape, like an oval sphere of light moving through his bloodstream. If he could continue this moment indefinitely, the sight of her back as she walks briskly away—but while time at the subatomic level is sometimes reversible, time at our level marches on. She goes into the grill, lusting after that sandwich.

Scene II

"I'm in love with Laura." Saying it as one might say I wish I were rich. Manuelo looked amused.

"She does not vant you, my friend," André said as tenderly as possible. "She does not vant anee of us."

"She deserves a prince," Manuelo burst out. "She's not interested in a virgin," he added as though there were some score he knew.

"Leesen my friend, theese eese folly."

"Uh-huh," Brian agreed, wishing for once folly might sweep him up out of logic and calculus into the improbable. He looked at André, a helpless look: save me! (But we tried!) In the crunch he was too intelligent not to fall in love with her.

Though he needs to prepare for the Harvard and MIT interviews.

Though she is unattainable.

André told her. When he told her, she thought well of Brian. He has, she thought, the imagination to desire the impossible.

What could be worse than denying oneself a romantic life?

Prison.

Torture.

Early cancer.

The hard labor of the poor in third world countries.

But this is Stanford, not São Paulo. She must struggle to rise—there's nowhere to go but up. He must concentrate simply to stay level—the thrust of Science has already shot him into the upper atmosphere and shows no sign of deceleration.

Scene III

He calls her. What the hell.

"This is Brian," he says. "Look, I'd like to talk to you. Could you go out for dinner tonight? It really would mean a lot to talk to you." Coming from the king of the frat house this speech would be just another line. You pause, though when such a speech is delivered by a real, suffering man in the world.

"Well," she says, laughing, "you are direct."

"How else can I be with you under the circumstances. Listen, I just want to talk to you. We've never actually talked you know."

"I want to be straight with you," she replied. "I can have dinner, that would be fun. But I don't know if André told you I'm in love with someone. I don't know if he told you that." Both of them know this is a lie told to save face for both of them.

"He didn't, but I'll accept that. I'll pick you up at six, then, if six is all right."

They meet frequently.

How does this happen? Brian keeps proposing they meet, Laura keeps accepting his proposals. They stick to the rule that Laura's in love with someone else, therefore their meetings are platonic. Brian talks, Laura listens patiently. She is so forbearing, deals with him so delicately, that he begins to feel encouraged. Her patience resonates with such benign intent that he is very nearly moved to shouts. He decides to take advantage of this, he'll take advantage of whatever there is. Brian talks, Laura listens, and a kind of steady state comes into being. Things get neither better nor worse. They meet but nothing comes of these meetings. The event of note is that they continue to meet. No meeting of theirs is the last meeting, each time the thrill that it isn't over yet. He gets to be a little whacko, she hasn't told him to buzz off. A little dizzy with the brashness of figuring what can he lose. So he begins to talk his love to her, he talks his life, tells her a novel, trying to build up sympathy for the main character. He takes pains not to bore her, he works for eloquence, lacing his tale with as much panache as he can. For weeks he talks her up, developing fluency, embellishing the basic theme with mad little forays into the ridiculous. He says some fairly bizarre things. "My system hasn't been prepared for you, my system's been prepared for a paper towel." "If I could fuck you just once." "Marry me."

She answers patiently. "I can't marry you. You know I'm not in love with you, I can't pretend otherwise."

He's wildly happy; when she speaks, he devours her reasonable replies. Everything she says is completely reasonable, he doesn't disagree with her for a minute. He appreciates her honesty, he appreciates her agreeing to listen to him. He appreciates her sitting still and letting him look at her day after day. My God, the privilege! None of the others get this privilege; she meets only him in this oddly intimate way. Yes, he thinks, they are intimate! Their friends observe them and make no comment, move a little away, as though to give them privacy. No one, not even Manuelo, teases them. Brian thanks them from the bottom of his heart for shutting up. But it also scares him—if they harassed him he'd remember there is no hope, he'd remember to take this lightly. But they are most pointedly not harassing him. It's as though each friend is privately holding his breath, pretending to be going about business as usual, but actually staring wide-eyed. Like physicists examining an S matrix, their adrenaline shoots up, just watching. They wish Brian well, they go on not breathing for his sake. He gets tearful at the thought of their friends' hopefulness. He and Laura work at encouraging the tendency for hope to exist, to actually exist. He pours his heart and soul into their mutual endeavor. Their effort will not fail on *his* account! To accomplish this he builds onto the edifice of their conversation, and at the same time his brain continuously monitors the keeping of his cool. Get sleep, don't drink too much, think tall, eat slow, read Marx, don't turn around fast.

As for Laura, she is obliged to sip a lot of things slowly. Coffee, orange juice, bourbon, whiskey sours, Manhattans, lemonade, glasses of water. She seems always to have a glass before her. Life takes place at a series of tables and on each table a glass of liquid she is obliged to drink. She has agreed to listen, she has agreed to take him seriously. When and how did she agree to this? Well, she doesn't want to hurt his feelings, there's that. Though she has turned and walked away from bleeding men without a backward glance. She wonders about this, is forced to conclude that she actually has begun to like listening to him. She finds she gets interested: what amazing remark will next fall from his lips? Though he began awkwardly, he is developing a new genre, and this form is for her, exclusive: such talk no one else will hear. His talk is made especially for her, a custom job, impressive in its inventiveness, its volume. When she knew him casually he seemed bookish and flabby. Now he has shown her his brilliance! Fiery tongues! The frankincense and myrrh of the soul! If he were already Einstein she might be tempted. Einstein was a sexy man at fifty, it's the early stages of genius that are repulsive. Like wine, genius has to age properly. Still, she is moved by Brian's predicament, a man trapped in a fat kid's body. And no one else has offered her intimacy. She begins to understand that no one else has spoken seriously to her before.

Painful Paradox, Part I

She acknowledges to herself that they *are* intimate.

Painful Paradox, Part II

Precisely this intimacy makes their union impossible. Think about it: why shouldn't she go to bed with him, give him her present? She does with plenty of other men she's not in love with. She toys with them, they toy with her, and in the great scheme of things all parties are innocent, no one gets ripped off.

But to toy with this man would be an atrocity!

She must *not* go to bed with him, precisely because she isn't in love with him.

A party in the Palo Alto hills, somebody's parents' house, the parents gone. Evening in May, air soft, abundance of flora in the deepening dark. Nature doing the pants-off things. Increasingly black sky, increasingly star-studded. Radio sources in distant galaxies beaming their beams to the scene. The quarter moon, sharp as a die, this moon enough to make even Brian shut up.

They wander out to the flagstone terrace, Brian brings along a bottle of Scotch. She feels like she's in an ad for Chanel, a beige silk dress, understated, very classy. The future hasn't shown up, but she's ready. Goes out occasionally with some man who looks promising but isn't. This interlude is all right with her though, everyone is required to put up with a certain amount of dead time. Meanwhile she's amused carrying on negotiations with Brian. Like two nations engaged in talks, they can't simply walk away, go about business. They must reach agreement on the issues, neither can face their constituencies without a treaty. They do not touch, but act as though they do (or do they act as though they don't but do?). They stand a little away from the others, they're at the party but not at the party. "You know I'm in love with you," Brian begins. A winning case begins with a summary of the basics. He continues casually, a bit methodically at first, but as he drinks he begins to extemporize, he begins to talk in earnest. "Listen Laura, I've got this idea. It's really very simple: we lie down side by side on a bed, and what we do then is stare up at the ceiling. Nothing tricky about this at all, trust me. No strings attached, we don't even hold hands—unless of course you wanted to—but in my view the situation is basic. We lie completely still and stare at this ceiling. Absolutely no lust present, I swear it. I do not get hard, we stay chaste as brother and sister. Flat on our backs, we don't even look at each other. Don't turn your head! The point is this ceiling over both of us at once, and at which we are both of us staring up at the same time. We stare at this ceiling at the same time! Synchronicity, Laura! Think what I'm saying! It costs you nothing, you don't have to compromise your principles, you go right on believing in love as though nothing unusual is happening, I go right on not turning so much as the flickering of an eyelash in your direction. . . ."

His speech begins to slur, she listens patiently. She intends to perform her task to the best of her ability. He lurches on with this line of rhetoric, beginning to sway where he stands. She tries to see his eyes through the thick lenses, but what she sees is a seething mass of talk, a buzz of subatomic events emitting sound. She has the perception suddenly that he really has lost his boundaries, has become pure sound hovering about her. He has dispersed, and the drone of his talk is now just part of everything, that landscape that is everywhere around her.

"Christ," he says then, "I'm going to be sick."

Oh no. She's suddenly on call, slings his arm over her shoulder. André sees them and hurries over, slips under Brian's other arm.

"You should not dreenk, my friend," he admonishes, but Brian doesn't hear, is already deeply into misery. Inside and upstairs they find a bedroom, moonlit, stagger forward, lunge, lay him down. André motions to Laura to stay with Brian, says, "I veel geet a pan."

She stands over Brian, as though keeping watch. What is it she watches over? His ruined childhood? His stuttering soul? He moans and jerks. She touches his shoulder, but he is too far gone to notice her hand. Light from that moon pours a stream across the carpet, pure milk of the spiral arms. She observes this light as a sweet invitation to enter even further everything there is. And she is about to kneel, intending to speak to him, bring him to his senses, when he twists up, and in one grand unmistakable arcing, leans over, throws up at her feet.

The sound of his retching, she feels, is more of her task, she listens to this patiently too.

Later, very late, when the party breaks up, she goes back to the bedroom, looks in. André washed the carpet with soapy water, but the room still smells faintly of vomit. The moon has moved on, leaving a trickle of itself thin as a length of string at the foot of the bed. Brian snores. She thinks she will wake him, then changes her mind, lies down beside him instead, takes his hand. She can feel his fingernails bitten to the quick, poor baby. Side by side, their bodies, impossibly cruel, oh very cruel, she thinks, the housings of souls. Who planned this, she wonders, who set us up? His snore reminds her of something large and reeking of itself, a woolly mammoth, maybe, or a Gaudi cathedral full of old pizza. She holds his hand, but after a moment he jerks in his sleep, and flops over, away from her.

She stays, looking up at the ceiling, memorizing the shadows, remembering for him.

Superluminal Speed

Before she publicly announces her engagement, Laura calls Brian one evening to tell him. "I've been expecting it," he manages. "Congratulations." Gets off the phone as fast as he can. Rushes out, gets behind the wheel, puts the key in the ignition.

He sits behind the wheel.

He knew someday he would have to marry Beth. Beth is the real world, and he has been mad. Destructive, crazy, romantic madness! His dreadful life rises up mocking, and he begins to fall—no, plunge—downward to depression. He who was going levelly about his business, memorizing theorems, plodding eastward across the tundra. But he can't get depressed, he can't stop studying, this would mess up his prospects, ruin what life he has. His life depends on maximum output, depression is a luxury he can't afford. His teeth clench, his jaw locks, his blood pressure shoots up, and he bursts into tears.

He sits behind the wheel, sobbing. Stars, one by one, come out above him.

Status Quo Update

Spring rains have given way to sunny days, bathing suits, magnolia-scented twilights. He tries doggedness to get back in the groove. He tries to get interested in Beth, goes through all the motions. He proposes, she accepts. Presto, he finds himself engaged. He even attempts to ravish her on the seat of his car, but in the process of getting himself ready he panics. What in God's name is he doing! He doesn't want her! "Listen, I'm sorry," he says. "We really should wait. I know you want to wait and you're right. We'll wait." Working at feeling affectionate, he kisses her hair. Actually Beth would like not to wait, but decides to go along with Brian. She's ready to leap out of blouse, bra, skirt, and panties, but she thinks it best, now, not to tell him. This decision should come from the man in her judgment. She pulls up short, and he is relieved, his penis soft, declining flesh. Maybe later, this infatuation with Laura passé, later when he and Beth are actually married.

Then, surely, he will rise.

GOOD-BYE GANG

He has not got over the mortification of having passed out in her presence. He determines to rise above this sordid event, to rise so high and so magnificently that the image of his disgrace will disappear so thoroughly it will actually never have existed. His wish is simple: to annihilate unflattering portions of the past. Such is his will in this matter that the impossible poses no obstacle. He intends to make an impressive final impression. She'll remember him as a man, dammit, a person with intelligence, dignity, sophistication. He has planned this final meeting, the aplomb with which he will conduct himself. He's even planned his parting words to her, the expression on his face when he delivers them. "Look," he says on the phone, "I want to say good-bye. But not on the phone. Let me take you out, we'll have a celebratory drink."

"Oh good," she says, enthusiastic, "I'd love to." She's relieved actually, he sounds sane, she hears him gathering himself into a semblance of poise. Not bleeding after all, no reason she need feel guilty. When André told her Brian and Beth were engaged, she envied them the simple curve of their lives. Only for a moment, though—after all, it wasn't her curve. She thinks hers is the one she will travel with John, and she is not completely full up with the fact of him—his handsome confidence, his position at HEW, his lust for her, his intention to run for high office. They'll move to the capital, she'll wield her French for profit, they'll make money and love, ascend and ascend. With this infusion of euphoria she has become even more attractive. Strangers who meet her on the street stare, wondering how she got that way. Now this one last loose end will be tied up: no ugly scene with Brian, no sad silence between them. He's measuring up, he's coming around. She sings to herself as she brushes her hair.

The patio of some bar or other. Laura's silk dress will survive the *Sturm und Drang* of fashion. She looks glittering, a scene out of *Breakfast at Tiffany's*. He orders champagne to mark the occasion. He wants to get just a tiny bit drunk, enough to enjoy to the bittersweet hilt this last cluster of moments with her. This after all is their last meeting, this is the meeting that will ring the change. They reminisce and laugh, they toast each other's engagements. She says she'll write, thinking he'll like that, but he waves this away, I can make it on my own thanks. She's impressed by this savoir faire, and she wishes him well. She who has, at the moment, all the advantages.

They leave, sunniness of afternoon over them. She notices his hands on the wheel, remembers feeling the tips of his fingers. His fingernails have not grown out. She hasn't really looked at him, she has thrown her whole being into listening, dimming out his visual presence. It occurs to her to wonder if he's feeling so fine as he professes, and she begins to suspect that in fact he's making a heroic effort. He looks under strain, as though the thinnest of spines may at any moment fail to hold him upright. And then it hits her: she's been avoiding her feelings. How to dismiss their strange tenderness, their intimacy like no other event in the galaxy! To think that he actually wanted to marry her! The passion in him! The things he said! Marriage would be a disaster, she thinks, she'd go mad. And she never intended this, their being duped, led on by some force mocking them both, a great cosmic joke at their expense. But if nothing in this universe is casual, why in the hell did she suppose *she* could be? He's part of my history, she thinks, his dye in the cells of her memory attesting to his having been there. Like parents and kin, he is a chemical fact in her, in her blood, in her chromosomes, in her spiraling DNA. Well she will not let him be ruined, she loves him! She cares about his goddamn soul!

He imagines the moment when he will leave the motor running, possibly a quick kiss on the cheek, then she will wave as he drives away waving. When he pulls up she says, "Turn off the motor."

"I'll go on," he says, not wanting to lose the pretty illusion of having a grip. "Come in," she says, "I want to take you to bed with me. Yes," she says, "you heard me rightly." And she turns from him, slides toward the door. Water torture, needles under the fingernails. All right, he gets out, his body seems to be working. He can, after all, stand up, he can walk. He stands and walks, one foot in front of the other. And bringing to the moment as much grace as he can muster, he follows her up the steps, inside.

She pours Scotch into glasses. He's clumsy with the ice, but this is reassuring, he still has his quavering hold on things. And he observes his own clumsiness for the first time as benign: she doesn't mind it. She leans against the counter, calm, opening all his doors, letting the sun stream in. Whatever he does is all right—hasn't she been telling him this, hasn't she been agreeing to him for weeks now, for months?

He goes to her, kisses her on the mouth. She opens her mouth, inviting his tongue inside. He explores this mouth of hers, pulls her against him, discovers his prick already rising—what should the order of events be! He kisses her again, she seems to like it! His hand rhythmically squeezing her shoulders, one hand down her spine, slow trepidation, oh God the cheek of her ass in his hand!

When he pulls away to look at her she takes him into another room.

The bed. His consciousness catapults forward—will he survive the sight of this bed? The spread is white, he will never forget this. She squeezes his hand, letting him get used to things, and he's encouraged: he'll forge ahead! She has to help him a little with her buttons, but he steels his nerves and all by himself pulls away one strap of her brassiere, revealing her lovely tit, Kodacolor. He stares at her breast for seconds and more seconds, trying to go slowly memorize the detail. The seconds tick and gather around them, steady and quiet, sparrows assembling. What, he wonders, can she be thinking, just as she leans, lifting her nipple to his mouth.

Take anything at all that's offered, anything! He closes his eyes and gently sucks, hears her breathing, listens to it change. Hears her fingernails growing, her hair humming, the sound of a struck tuning fork coming off her skin. He stops to draw breath, she takes off her dress, skirt a blossom opening around her shoulders. Naked, gleaming like the gold of Tutankhamen, she kneels, begins to unlace his shoes. A voice in his head shouts: she's naked at your feet! Where did she learn such things, think up this devastating simplicity! He watches her perform the miraculous act of undoing the buttons of his shirt. The sordid details of undressing, he discovers, are practiced movements in an act of devotion. Her tiniest motions take on the weight of rite, and she proceeds to unbuckle his belt. Obediently he stands, and when she looks up he feels his knees go weak: SHE IS NOT DOING THIS OUT OF KINDNESS.

Adrenaline, buckets of it, racing around in him. He pulls her to her feet. She is at once so tensile and so pliable in his hands that he wants to weep. He lays her down, gets out of his pants and shorts, oh God to lie down naked beside her, that would be enough, can he stand more? Yes, but he is not going to be able to be slow, he's had no practice at controlling this careening feeling, and he climbs up and pushes his thickened penis into her—easily, gloriously—he knows what to do after all! Suddenly everything is pure physics—as she reaches up with her hips, as he delves, space-time expanding in every direction, Bell's Theorem proving and proving, and as it proves, the thought comes to him that he'll never need even a glass of water again.

Bell's Theorem suggests that what we think of as separate parts of the universe are intimately, immediately, connected. Brushing her hair one morning years later she thinks of him. An ordinary enough January day, elms leafless and black, the temperature dropping. Her husband (the second) has already left for his office. She hears her son running water in the bathroom, her daughter talking to the cat as she fills its bowl.

Laura stands in her slip at the full-length mirror, brushing her hair, considering this hair of hers critically. She is letting it grow long again, and as she brushes she admires the length, its fullness and color, a few strands of gray making their premiere appearance. *A gorgeous head of hair still*, she thinks, and flips backward to *then* and him, Brian: *what did my hair look like back then?* It wasn't curly, for one thing, this waviness set in after the birth of her daughter, her coming permanently altering her mother's chemistry. Back then, she realizes, we rang each other's changes. His talk not idle talk and her listening not lost on him. And his speeches still a part of him now, as her decision to act that sunny afternoon has been present ever since, a throbbing in sinew and bone. Only the particular curve of their tenderness—his talk and her listening, his drunken lack, her soft fullness—could have produced her as she is, here, now, before this mirror.

She supposes one day when she's an old woman she will open the newspaper and read the announcement of his prize.

And she brushes her hair and thinks very well of him. She brushes her hair and thinks very well of herself.

The Fur of the Bear

It comes up in you big, for sure, like your face in the mirror. The way a drug comes up when it takes you, grabbing your breath. Up from your guts lungs heart, into the throat it comes, filling the vessels in the lining of your mouth with blood. You feel like a giant lily's opening around you. And you're big, very big, bones and hair growing. Chest back and nerves, hair, skin knuckles blood. You have hooves you have hide you have tusks you have nostrils.

I sit drinking tea, leaning on the sill, looking down. People sitting in cafés, people streaming on sidewalks. Going up and down stairs, people, their moving their talking. Morning, dawn of civilization. You think sometimes it's cool, just sitting and watching, that you're outside it, you can watch it go by. Then you notice your heart beating faster, your eyes and hearing going faster, throbbing.

When you don't want to know there's this something inside you, you look away—for a while it will leave you alone. Turn, go back down, lie curled in your belly. Wait, try to get smaller, sleep. You can tame it, teach it tennis or cards. Teach it manners. Train it to wait outside. You can throw away clothes, lamps dishes, old papers. Burn books, pour the booze down the toilet. You can stay home, you don't have to move, train yourself to sit still, make your eating slow. Or keep moving, it's the same thing as stillness. Take a vow, change jobs. Sell your car, have children.

You can do it for a while—keep it quiet, work your way around it. It's there, but you can make it sleep for a while. Then a day comes when you can't pretend you don't have it, when it comes up bigger than you ever knew you were. Try crying, twist, stuff your own hands in your mouth. Swallow something: metal, rubber, ground glass. But it's there and now it won't, it won't sleep.

This animal you wish they'd asked you if you wanted.

Wind in the leaves. Leaves in the grass. *Jane*. In me something that was is continuing. It's like wearing a silk skirt, where you go it goes with you, smoothness humming over your skin.

You think nothing happens? Everything happens. It's March now it's November it's August it's May. Leaves at the window, a branch tapping. A wasp sits still on the mantel, then walks.

A basket, this pillow, a glass of water, napkins.

Water evaporating from the surface of water.

Light across the bed, slant across my knee, my thigh. The tick of time is warmer than many ovens. The handle of the cupboard door, the heat of many hands in it. On the floor my shoes, taking the shape of my feet. Plants making chlorophyll, insects hovering. The smell of my own skin is like no other.

I was humming to myself, I had plans, then he stepped through that doorway. Said my name, *Jane*, up at the end like a question. Smiling a little, like maybe he knew me. I didn't know him but he seemed to know me. His body filling the doorway, light coming from behind.

I couldn't quite see him with the light behind him. Light around his body, around him like color. I couldn't quite take in the distinctness of his features. And I didn't quite want to look directly at him. I was afraid if I really looked it would hurt me. Like they tell you don't look straight at the sun.

Once when I touched him he pretended he didn't feel it. He didn't want to feel it. He pretended he didn't notice. Though my heat shot through his arm he wanted to refuse it. He pretended not to know why I was angry.

"You turn your back," I said. "So now get off me. Let go my hand, my foot. Let go my nipple. Get off my belly, you're sitting on my head."

My bare foot on the floor, real as a fish on smooth wood.

Then it came up in me. My hands sweating, the wings of my shoulders fluttering, the front of my body quivering, breath beating me like a skin drumhead. I reached out for his hands, his face, I reached for his shoulders. I took in his thighs, his liver his lungs his ears. I reached for his wrists, to hang on, I reached for his ribs, a handful. I took hold of his belt, reached all the way through to his spine. The air around us red, a thick skin of red light. A pulse. The brain burning purple, then blue, burning through the spectrum. Burning and moving on through, peeling off color after color. You could see through my hand, I saw light through my ankle. The skin of my belly startling, glowing like plankton at night. My heart cooking blood, my eyes making mercury. More and more light kept welling up out of me. I kept hearing my name, he kept repeating my name to me. My name, burning through me like a laser. A laser piercing my soul. I have a soul.

Every time we meet someone the blades of the fan spin. The light burns faster. There's sky through a window. Shadows on the walls then are like no other shadows. A phone. The rattle of a typewriter. A girl in a purple blouse walks by the open window. The roar of a bulldozer. A potted fern. People on sidewalks, people at crossings. Someone calls out your name. You turn.

If you lay your ear against someone's belly you don't hear the steady, predictable heart. You hear something else, slaps and great churnings, the whole works colossal, a roaring, then quiet. Long passages and turnings, a windy air whistling. Some god mouth stuttering.

Even the bear's fur makes a sound.

Even if you lie still everything happens. A faucet dripping, a dog yapping. A woman's voice, and a child answering, anemones by the steps, their many colors ticking ticking. If you try to hold the moon it goes down while you watch it. Turn on the faucet, water down the drain. Stare at the floor and the light passes over you. Lie still and you feel your hair growing.

The toad in the foot is there, the lizard in the jaw. You feel your hair growing and you want to celebrate. The brain's thrumming gets louder as you go with its moving, as you walk toward someone coming toward you in the cloud of their moving as you come toward them. You keep walking, that's the thing, you keep walking. You go right toward them, straight into the pupil, which dilates wide to receive you, and then reverses, squeezes shut behind you, contracts, closes like the mouth of a womb.

You think you know things and then you don't know them. Once in a blizzard it snowed in through an open window. I'd been working, I'd gone to sleep exhausted. I woke up and found thick white flakes piling on the bed.

You can die sitting still. If you go out you drown. Take drugs or don't. There are no ideas. Take drugs or don't. Either way you're alive. Two little kids, building in the sand, with water. Stacking the wet sand, patting it in place. Bring the drips over here, she says, over here. He does. Bigger and bigger, up, the spire of their castle. In the moat they float catalpa blossoms. They sail catalpa leaves for boats.

Sometimes the gods stick a little knife in and turn it. Sometimes they send money. Sometimes nothing. Whatever happens you have this animal with you. And a little silver key turns the soft doors open again.

Something Unforgivable

Price had his bad moments. At the Comstocks he'd got into one of those moments, inadvertently and apropos of nothing in particular, except perhaps that he was envious of the man, Will, about whom he began to tell the story. That, and the amount he'd drunk. They had ordered bourbons before dinner, he and Pat, and when the Comstocks, whom they hadn't seen for a year or so, appeared, they had asked the couple to join them. The four of them had gone on drinking with dinner, and all of them drank more than they might have ordinarily, caught up in the occasion of their chance meeting. Afterward at the Comstocks all of them had a cognac while Sarah made espresso. Price had one cognac and then another. And there had been an air of celebration about the evening, and the renewal of their suspended acquaintance led Brad to go the little extra and bring out the mirror, separate the white powder into four equal portions. He did this with a detectable flourish, as if to say the occasion called for the best and a little more. Pat and Sarah declined lines, but there they were, so their husbands had each done two. When Sarah carried in the tiny cups of coffee, Price, animated, was launching the anecdote about Will.

The volume of his voice rose like a record someone turns too high and walks away from. By sheer superior energy he took over the room, seizing its objects to himself, appropriating the three of them as an audience. He sat up very straight on the edge of the couch, happy with his sudden unforeseen command of things. Facing Brad, he found he was terribly pleased with Brad's face, and with Brad's eyes on him, attentive and patient. He would give Brad this anecdote the way a man gives another a cigar, an act that serves to bind them, confirming the link of their masculinity. And he would do this, knowing that when the cigar is superior, it also confirms the precedence of the giver.

"This is *the* quintessential Will story," he said. "The true mark of the man revealed by his own hand." There was in his tone a condescension he did not detect, wound as he was on his talk, talk which he was feeling was excellent and satisfying, talk of the calibre of the Courvoisier warming him with its sterling fire. "Pat's a fan of Will's," he continued, waving his cigarette, "but she hasn't heard this yet." Price intended to acknowledge his wife's presence, to include her and by extension Sarah, too, in the conversation.

Pat was neither a fan of Will's nor was she not. The man was simply someone she knew, one of Price's colleagues at the office. She had met Will and they had talked briefly on one or two occasions. She scarcely knew him well enough to have an opinion about his character. But she said nothing. She sat beside Price, holding the tiny cup and saucer, anticipating the evening's continuous unfolding. She supposed her husband was about to tell an amusing story.

It was then the moment engulfed him. One moment he was in control of things and the next moment he had lost the thrust of his narrative completely. Though he was unaware of forgetting, he suddenly forgot to tell the story he intended to tell. All he said and continued to say was preliminary to the anecdote itself, introductory phrases repeating, spinning like a wheel in mud. He talked energetically, his delivery circling back on itself and him, encircling him, running over and through him repeatedly in only very slight variations. His voice rose higher still on its own excitement, and on the excitement of the drama he imagined he was unfolding.

Pat withdrew, her gaze floating idly from object to object—the Farouk, Sarah's face, the exquisitely small cup in her hand. She had learned, when trapped by a tedious speaker, to turn the moment to advantage by escaping into the visual. When Price paused, she spoke. "What did Will do?" she asked, hoping to release him into his story. Once the tale got going the evening could be rescued. The story itself would be entertaining; Price was good at telling amusing stories. And then the story would end, the conversation move on. They would be spared embarrassment. They would all visit together. "What did he do?" she repeated.

"I'm getting to that," Price said, emptying the snifter. He slammed the glass bottom down with emphasis. At times he felt he had finally found his rightful place in the world. He felt this now, and he noticed that his body along with his mind had expanded to fill quite an imposing space. He was happily surprised by the magnitude of this and by the stunning skillfulness of his presence in the Comstocks' livingroom. He imagined existence welcoming him in all his magnificence, imagined he was close as a man could get to the spinning hub of the universe. He himself was the *prima facie* evidence that he deserved everything, and more. He plunged on.

"Say, Price," Brad interrupted, gesturing as if to imply *peace, be still, I have something to say you won't want to miss*. But Price at just that moment stood up and crossed to the mantel. He would address them from there. He turned toward them, but as he turned, an old suspicion he had forgotten surfaced—the suspicion that once at a party this Will had managed some intimacy with Pat, a real, invading intimacy. As he remembered it Pat had been flirting openly with Will very, very late at night in someone's garden—whose? He remembered the lighted garden—torches burning or Chinese lanterns hung from the trees—and then the light dwindling off into darkness at the edges. The two of them, Will and Pat, at the edge of the light, talking animatedly, laughing, gesturing. Will lighting her cigarette, reaching up and lifting something—a petal?—from her hair. An infuriatingly intimate gesture, and Price, caught in a less than casual conversation, could not leave to move toward them, to stop the man's brash liberties. While Price watched they had turned and wandered off into the dark, the man Will placing his arm casually around Pat's shoulder as they walked away, as though to suggest they were only close friends (when had they become close friends!), the kind of gesture made to cover very different feelings, intentions. At some point they had both appeared again, Pat in the house talking to the family's teenage daughter, and Will on the other side of the garden. Price had proceeded to get very drunk, and he and Pat had never spoken of the evening. It occurred to Price now that something unforgivable had happened that night. A blow he had never acknowledged had struck him. He, who deserved the best treatment, had been treated shabbily.

Pat had stopped listening, and she had crossed her legs away from his seat on the couch. She was uncomfortable, though she felt Price's actions rightfully had nothing to do with her. She was a separate creature, not accountable for him, but because he was her husband she wished to God he would stop embarrassing himself. She felt sorry for him, stunned and blinded as he was, but she was impatient, too, since he was beginning to ruin what had begun as a fine evening for all of them. His predicament, she felt, was entirely his fault. Still, she determined to take the situation lightly. He was, after all, a good husband. He had his bad moments, but not often.

Then he was before her, still standing, directing the energy of his body—the accumulated resources of his innermost being—directly and unmistakably toward her. "Now, Pat," he said, "takes Will very seriously. She is in fact quite dazzled, a sort of Will groupie, my wife. His façade glitters, and Pat is blinded by the light. She succumbs and drops to her knees."

She could not believe he had actually said this. Had he said this? She was irritated but did not react. She was determined now to make light of whatever happened. Besides, it was clear that he was fascinated with his talk, the phenomenon of talk, that what he wanted was simply to go on talking until he ran down. Later she remembered Brad had stood up too. Maybe he had tried to talk Price down by sheer force? Brad was the taller, and it was conceivable Price might have been intimidated by another man posed in front of him. She remembered the two of them standing, shouting, waving their arms. She had ignored them and carried on a conversation with Sarah. When their children were babies, Sarah had once given Pat baby clothes her child had outgrown, tiny sweaters and sleepers and booties, and Pat, remembering this now, used it to reinforce the link between them. At some point Sarah rose and opened the door to the patio, and Pat joined her. They stood on the threshold, talking, looking out at the stars.

Pat had said then that she and Price must get their jackets, they must go. Sarah suggested meeting for lunch, she and Pat, and Pat agreed cheerfully. And somehow then they had gone. She had felt the greatest relief, getting Price into the car.

He would probably not remember the next day what he had done.

He woke feeling dread. Pat was still asleep, her breathing barely detectable. He lay very still, not ready to see her open eyes looking into his. He did not want to wake so soon. Existence brought forth the unexpected, and a person needed time to prepare. They should not spring surprises on a man, he thought.

The evening before appeared now in his memory as a generalized fuzziness shot with images of attempted camaraderie. Had they been successful, those attempts? He did not connect the evening with his present sense of foreboding. His perception of dread seemed to spring spontaneously out of the present, and in fact he felt dreadful. He ached, and he assiduously desired unconsciousness: complete blankness and total inactivity in all the circuits of his brain. But his brain was already clicking away, and he lay, helplessly letting it run on, hoping for a glimpse of the shape his foreboding might take. Then, deciding it was no use, he sat up, moving slowly, taking care not to disturb Pat.

Downstairs he cut a lemon in half and squeezed the juice into a glass. He added pressed garlic and olive oil, the remedy for hangover. What this was designed to do was flush out the liver. The recipe had been given him by a buddy in college, and Price followed it faithfully, ritually. If he could get this right, the proportions of the remedy, he felt things—all things, things in general—would be well on the way to improving. He swirled the potion, keeping his attention centered on this motion, and drank it down. It tasted not unpleasantly like salad dressing. This taste, heralding normality, usually made him feel improved. It pleased him to think that these simple elements—lemon, olive oil, a clove of garlic, these pure forms—could relieve terror.

He stood at the kitchen counter, waiting for the magic to take effect. In the backyard two starlings squawked, walking stiffly in the grass. The mother directed her squawk at the fledgling, hopping beside this baby, lecturing, giving advice and encouragement. She was surely admonishing her child, encouraging it to gird its loins and attempt flight. Price remembered his mother filling a bowl with Wheaties for him. Was he six? Seven? Breakfast of Champions. Wheaties and milk, and now the virtues of milk—its protein, its calcium, how if you could choose only three foods for the rest of your life one of them should be milk—all this lore came back to him. His mother had reminded him of the wonders of milk as she filled his bowl. She filled him with milk and with milk facts, and each day she had encouraged him again to try his wings.

Price studied the pair of birds now with a penetrating scrutiny. His mother had assumed he would prosper, she had groomed him for success. She'd believed he was bound for glory of some kind. She had done her part, just as this mother bird now hopped about encouragingly, willing her baby to command his own resources. But the dumb bird wasn't flying. Hopelessly lumpy—or was it the scruffy feathers that made it seem so?—the poor thing squawked and ran a few steps and flapped its wings but did not come anywhere near taking off.

This omen struck Price in his softest place. He realized his sense of doom on waking had been right and accurate, a true perception. He was not succeeding as his mother had supposed he would. A truth about himself he had refused to acknowledge arrived in his consciousness and refused to be dispelled: his job, commanding an office, pushing paper, was a job anyone could do. He had not lived up to his potential, he felt this now. That they were well enough off seemed beside the point. It had been easy to make money in this way, he thought, and he had done the easy thing.

He had done the easy thing, though it was not what he was suited for, this job anyone could do. He had been meant to do something else with his life, something specifically his. And he had failed: he had not even tried to discover what it might be. He had gone through motions, he had learned moves. He had learned to look good. But it was sleight of hand; he had become skilled at sleight of hand. He was no more than a wheel spinning in place. He had not commanded his resources. He had simply gone forward in the footprints of others.

At that moment Pat came downstairs. She had sat up in bed, cross-legged, like the Indians sat before their fires—so her grandmother had told her when she was four—and noticed, on the inside of her thigh near the knee, the new pink line of an artery beginning to break. And she had experienced a rush of satisfaction, of elation. She was getting older, yes, here was another sign, and it wasn't at all terrible. On the contrary, she was aging happily and well. She could feel the immensity of the good years still before her, how she would come into them gracefully and in due time. She had put the previous evening out of mind, and she was filled with a sleepy zest, happy to be waking. She decided she would wear a pair of shorts and her favorite red halter top. The idea of the red top filled her with cheerfulness. She would put it on, and after coffee she would go to her desk and finish the letter she was writing to their daughter, who was away at school. She was pleased with the way she'd begun the letter, and she would be even more pleased, she knew, when it was finished and she sealed the envelope. The color red, the letter, lunch, gardening in the afternoon—there were so many, astonishingly many marvelous things to do in life.

She came up behind Price and put her arms around him, laying her cheek against his back. He did not move. He loved his wife, but it occurred to him now with a certain irony that there was nothing special about this love of his. Anyone else could do as well, or better. He had no idea how he might have loved her, if he had lived differently, if he had fulfilled his mother's hopeful expectations. He could not imagine what he might have been, and what he might now become seemed already determined. However much he might will himself to change, the circuits of his brain would insist on their patterns. Surely the tracks of these circuits were deeply grooved, dogged tracks. He could not imagine learning to think differently. He did not believe he could learn to be other than he was.

No wonder when he woke he had willed his brain to shut down again. But it had not; it had insisted on processing its raw material, and now here he was. They should not spring surprises on a man, but they did. He could feel his liver, an ache, an overload. Perhaps he was no more now than a great weariness of the liver. The mother bird, keeping close to her baby, squawked again, and the baby flapped and wobbled. Price felt certain this dumpy bird could not possibly make it into the air—and if it did, its flight would be disjointed, faltering, a sore to the eye. Its wings were a hopelessly inefficient contraption, flopping first one way, then the other. Cursed with this apparatus, the creature's life would be ugly, Price thought, and filled with unremarkable events.

A short life. Or if long, then sadly, meaninglessly long.

Incapable of flight, he stood there. Pat hugged him, humming something airy, a tune that suggested the buzzing of dragonflies through summer air. When was it, he wondered, that he had given up milk? Maybe if he had stuck with milk, he thought disconsolately, his life might now be turning out differently. Who could tell what seemingly insignificant event tipped the balance, changed your life. He thought again of his mother then, and for a few moments he was deeply sorry for the waste of her affection on him.

Sons

What is it anyway with sons?   All my friends have them   and these friends of mine love these sons to distraction   These politically correct women comrades of mine   go ga-ga over their baby boys   They say *don't do that*   in a way that means go right ahead   Go right ahead and pull up those daffodils   Sweep a few dishes off the table   Go right ahead and poke your little friend's eyes out   Feel free to climb all over me   They let these sons walk all over them   as though their bellies, breasts, and shoulders are stairsteps   and the sons sit on their mother's heads kicking their mothers in the jaw   until finally their mothers smile and say *Sweetheart, you better get down now*

And do not try to have a conversation with these women while their sons are in the room or the next room   Sons do not want their mothers to have conversations   They climb up in their mothers' faces or bang them on the legs   demanding to talk, demand to be answered   demanding toys wound up and stories read   *Watch me!* they shout   And my friends smile as though all this is just cuteness   and cuteness is an accomplishment   and aren't they bright, these sons   All this beating on things and insisting adults be quiet   is a sign of brightness

These women are my friends, most of them militant feminists   who bust their asses for the ERA   drive two hours to hear Robin Morgan speak   and carry candles to take back the night   They go door to door for Safehouse   and they encourage men's groups   they have taken self-defense and karate They want day care centers and abortion rights and comparable pay for comparable worth   They set goals and work systematically toward them   They do not weep over the impossible   but go steadily ahead with the possible   They stuff envelopes and run meetings   organize conferences and serve on panels   They make the coffee   and they drink the coffee   and they get the referendum passed   They know the catechism   They wrote the catechism   They are handsome, smart, capable women And they will drop anything at all for their sons

Plus there is this pattern that their daughters are the oldest My friends, if they have two,   had girls first and then little boys   Now these girls are six and seven and eight,   old enough to get the picture   I watch them standing at the edge of things   When I go to Sharon's house Cybele stands back   She is thin and serious, an observer   of her mother and her brother Matthew   Sharon stands, heating the coffee   Matthew jerks at her skirt,   impatient, demanding jerks   talking loud and fast, banging her thigh   He demands Sharon attend his latest ruminations   with the utmost attention   and that she not go off and talk to me   and above all that she not notice Cybele Sharon has been promising Cybele attention with *just a minute, in a minute*   but Matthew demands Sharon deliver to him instead   all the attention she has   Cybele stands in her leotard, watching   dangerously thin, silent and seeing   Sharon is too busy to notice   This is what sons do, they keep you completely busy   Cybele   stands back and pines

"Cybele," I say, "I want to see your roundoff."   Cybele looks at me for the first time,   then back at her mother   I am not her mother   but I am someone Matthew doesn't have   In the livingroom she demonstrates her accomplishments,   roundoffs and perfect cartwheels   She is flushed, nervous but proud   She tells me her teacher thinks she is quick to learn   and she chatters on   until Sharon and Matthew appear in the doorway   Matthew just can't stand it   He rushes up and plops himself in my lap

"Matthew," I say, "please get down."   Cybele looks at me as though I've gone crazy   Sharon has a glazed look as she pours the coffee,   as though this is just the usual

As though nothing much is going on

I have lunch with my friend Helen   She looks beautiful and haggard today   We order wine with our smoked salmon omelets   Helen gets right into the wine, she's had it   She is troubled by her son Price,   Price who is three and monstrous   Price has completely cowed his six-year-old sister   He goes through her room systematically,   pulling books off the shelves and ripping out a few pages,   stamping on dolls like Atilla the Hun   And he purposely marches through her own little garden   stomping the shoots that have just come up   You can see Price will become Secretary of State,   making aggressive statements in the media,   demanding outrageous concessions from foreign countries,   grinding oppressed populations under his heel

Helen is a good woman,   intelligent and compassionate   She takes care of wallflowers at parties   and is nice to atrocious people   Treats everyone as though they have dignity and she can see it,   even the worst people   who haven't got a shred of dignity left   Helen thinks Idi Amin has dignity   and is just misguided   She believes in the First Amendment completely   and is never pissed off at Nazi parades, only troubled   She thinks if she could just talk to a few Nazis   and bring them to her house for coffee   they would realize their mistake   She is convinced we can all be friends here on the planet   And she really believes this   while I plot to murder Alexander Haig   and get vitriolic about the First   I think some people should be made to shut up   and if they would hire me to apply the First Amendment selectively   I could decide in a minute which ones should get it   But Helen believes in innate goodness   Like some believe in original sin   Helen believes in original good

Evil is just the result of a faulty environment

But now there is this problem of Price   who should be goodness itself, since he was raised   in a very exemplary environment   But he isn't good   Instead he throws himself at the world like a suicide pilot   Helen stands by,   pointing out in a reasonable voice   that what he is doing is wrong   Reason is her method   though with Price it just isn't working   Still she thinks that if she keeps talking to Price   in this reasonable voice   he will eventually heed her   The trouble is she thinks Price listens   Or will begin to listen sometime in the future

Actually Price hears nothing   but the wild cantering of his own little heart

Carolyn sends Charity to bed on schedule   She puts Darth down, too, but he cries   So she goes and gets him up, bawling bloody murder,   and brings him down to the livingroom   He looks at me, his mother's friend, and stops crying   Then he lunges out of Carolyn's arms   and parades around in front of us   pleased as punch to have our attention   When Charity comes down in her nightie, Carolyn is firm

"Charity, you get back in bed."   Darth is darthing away, smiling and waving at the crowd   Charity's face falls   You can see she thinks this is wildly unfair   She has to go back to bed because she's bigger and knows better   and Darth doesn't have to because he doesn't know better and is a baby   Only he isn't a baby, Charity thinks   He walks and talks like everyone else   He just pretends to be a baby   When, she wonders, will he know better?   Charity remembers being made to know better   a long time ago when she was very young

Carolyn asks Bill to put Darth back to bed   Bill takes Darth howling upstairs and Charity follows The howls go on and on Charity won't be able to sleep and Carolyn won't be able to relax She lights a cigarette and pretends to relax but you can see it's pretense She looks utterly wiped out but is dying to dash upstairs to Darth, Darth who made her tired in the first place He wants her and not Bill because he knows she will not be firm Sons do not like firmness They absolutely refuse it A homey softness is what they are after, as much of it as they can get

Now Carolyn smokes fast debating whether or not to bolt for the stairs

Is it heaven or hell to be wanted, I wonder when it's a son who wants you

I thought my mother was fair I did not feel she babied my brother too much I was eight when he was born and I babied him too I dressed him up and took him out in my wagon, pulled him down the street showing him off I was pleased to have this fat little baby to play with and I treated him like one of my dolls But actually my mother spoiled him a lot, or so my grandmother says My grandmother says I just didn't notice By the time my brother was four, she says, I had moon eyes for Gary Wiley and had left the real world temporarily but completely "I saw it coming," my grandmother says, "but I couldn't tell your mother a thing." And by the way, my grandmother should know She ruined a couple of my uncles herself One became an alcoholic though we had never before had one in the family The other never got it together to succeed at anything He was a handsome failure just like my brother is, and the brothers of my friends These brothers simply subsist, never amounting to much They run up outrageous medical bills getting malaria in the Peace Corps instead of getting the generator built Or they borrow money to start a hot tub business in a place where there are already hot tubs galore Helen, Sharon, and Carolyn excuse their brothers "My father was weak," Sharon says, "so Buddy didn't have a model." Maybe But Helen, Sharon, and Carolyn have strong husbands, two lawyers and a surgeon They are reasonable men and kind but they take no shit You have to say they are good models They love their kids but they are firm, when they're around

Which isn't much That's the thing, it's the mothers who are always around What I think happened to us, the sisters is our fathers were gone a lot, as is the practice of fathers and our mothers loved us but they had to live with us day in and day out You can get real tired of day in and day out So when we got to be impossible they let us have it We were not sons after all, just ordinary people and you don't baby ordinary people I was probably a monster at two whining and falling down in a fit, shrilly demanding cookies and lemonade at midnight, and screaming at my mother to watch me instead of watching her friend Betty My mother took it just so long Then she came and glared down at me "Marilyn," she said, "that's enough." And she whisked me up quicker than quick, swept outside and set me down on the porch "Marilyn," she said then, "don't you ever do that again."

My friends say their daughters were good girls and then they had sons and everything changed They don't say they changed They say everything changed Tess's son Alex who is three ripped all the paper curls off his sister Beth's unicorn piñata Beth was inconsolable She had been saving the piñata for her birthday and only when Tess got Beth's father to help paste it all back on could Beth stand up and go on with life "I don't think he meant any harm," Tess says "He just wanted to get at the candy which he probably thought was in there because I had said it wasn't."

Tess has heard about hyperactivity and she has decided Alex is hyperactive She watches his diet "He was getting too much sugar," she tells me Meanwhile Alex continues his program of genocide, pouring sand in the other kids' hair, pouring their soup into their very own laps and running head-on at the ones playing London Bridge, knocking down four or five at a time

Hyperactive is a convenient word Everyone thinks it has explained Alex's behavior It hasn't of course, it has only described it But it makes everyone feel better, except the kids with soup in their laps This word allows Tess to feel she has done all a mother can do and now her pediatrician has prescribed L-Tryptophan for Alex "An amino acid," Tess explains to me, "which acts as a relaxant." While we talk Alex crashes the salt and pepper shakers to smithereens and dumps a sack of sugar onto the carpet Then he takes Tess's glasses—one side in each hand—and neatly cracks the frame at the nosepiece.

His face is ruddy with guilty deliciousness at the sharp sound of the crack

I have only one friend who refuses to cave in to sons Her name is Mary but she is not a madonna by a long shot When Mary divorced Hardy's father Hardy was two and his sister five Maybe because Mary was the only parent she was very, very firm Once when I was visiting her, he whapped her on the leg with a piece of his erector set because she told him he had to put it away, every piece She swept him up to her eye level and shook him She looked him straight in the eye and said, "No!" He began to whimper and then to cry, one of those long drawn out wails of the mortally wounded Mary put him down, and said, "Tough, and don't even think about trying that again."

Now Hardy is eight, a spunky kid, bright-eyed and curious but obedient and polite He has never poured glue in anyone's hair, certainly not his sister's And he is quick to guess what Mary may want When she says, "Pick up that coat," he jumps to, lickety-split He toes the line, an abso-

lutely straight white line   And without being asked he checks
every night   to see if the trash needs taking out

All this is easy for me to say   I don't have a son   and
my daughters did what I said   They did not wreak destruc-
tion on the world around them   Though they ached to pick the
flowers, they did not   unless I said *yes, pick those sweet peas*
They only did terrible things to one another and to other children   when pushed to the limit   and then it was mostly
screaming and slamming of doors   If I had a son rattling the
bones of my nervous system,   driving trucks over people's
faces   and pouring Scotch down the sink to see it go   I'd probably go nuts   And his father would be no help at all   When the
girls were small   he hardly so much as told them   to stop arguing at the table   What in the world would he do with a son   A
son would probably bring us to divorce   two innocent people
just wanting to live and let live   and then we'd have a custody
battle,   the two of us fighting over our son   who had ruined
our marriage

My girls say to me, "You should have another baby, Mom,   because Dad needs a son."   They have never had a brother to com-
pete with   and so speak from a rosier viewpoint than some   I
don't want another baby   and neither does their father   but
they notice he has never actually said   he doesn't want a son
Not another kid to raise is how he puts it   But they are dying to
know where he stands on this matter   "Dad needs a son," they
say   and look to see how he will take this

Now that all of them have got safely through junior high   and
are old enough not to have to care

Now Carolyn reads in *Psychology Today*   that research has
been done proving conclusively   that boys like aggression for its
own sake   Aggression gives them a happy charge   but it
doesn't give girls a happy charge   Girls do not get vindictive for

no reason but boys get mad just because they like to To boys it feels good

Carolyn calls Tess to tell her and later calls the rest of us too That afternoon we go to Carolyn's house She makes margaritas and we munch guacamole It is like a summit meeting My friends are high on happiness At last they have found a reason why they can't manage their boys

I think of all those mornings with my friends, all those trips to the space capsule when we'd rather go to the botanical gardens, afternoons when the boys still need naps but are beginning to refuse to take them, evenings reduced to sentence fragments by little boys demanding drinks of water and then their older sisters begging for more goodnight kisses because their brothers are getting too many drinks all those times I ache to talk to my friends but can't pursue a line of thought for more than twenty seconds at a time We wait together through these times exchanging hopeful glances helplessly and hug each other goodbye with resignation We have not been able to visit but we are friends and we forgive each other, no matter how difficult, the conditions of our lives

So I have some more guacamole and I drink to this new, helpful research I drink with them and do not mention a certain experiment I watched on TV In this experiment mothers were asked to play ten minutes each with a girl and with a boy baby The boys were dressed as girls, and vice versa but the mothers didn't know this Now here's baby Valerie Mama holds Val on her lap "Aren't you pretty!" she says, over and over and she gives little Val a doll to play with, tells her to hold it close "Aren't you pretty!" the mother says "and such a good girl to hold the baby close!" She keeps Valerie on her lap the whole ten minutes

Now here's little Vince Mama reaches for a toy hammer She puts Vince on the floor on his belly and the hammer in front of him out of reach She coaxes him to inch forward, to crawl, to kick, to flail, anything to get that hammer

"Come on," she says, "you can do it!" She herself is on the floor, cheering working up enthusiasm you wouldn't believe

I drink to the bliss of ignorance And I drink secretly to my own good fortune If it happened to them it could happen to me But God did not pick me to be tested That one time God let me off He looked at me and said, *Let this one pass She couldn't take it and I don't want to be responsible Or worse, she wouldn't take it and would make a frightful scene calling in reporters and TV cameramen agitating all the other mothers getting up petitions and marching in the streets with banners and bullhorns, bringing the smooth, ongoing flow of world childcare to a halt Listen, I don't want that,* God said *Give her two or three daughters instead*

Mother

In the beginning there was my mother. A shape. A shape and a force, standing in the light. You could see her energy; it was visible in the air. Against any background she stood out. Heat radiating from her blurred objects as she moved past them so that it seemed her skin gave off a charge. Even sitting, writing a letter, sewing, or drinking a cup of coffee, she was kinetic, animated. They could have used her instead of Ready Kilowatt to see electricity. A buffer of radiance surrounded her, she gave off light.

My father was gone to the war. I was two and three and four, but I remembered him, checked my memory against the photograph on my mother's dressing table. A handsome man, though distant in the gilded frame, like the photograph of Clark Gable my mother kept on the other side. Two movie stars, from a realm not beyond but away, someplace I'd heard about but never seen, Tokyo, Guam, Hollywood, San Juan Capistrano. My father was not there to take me on the Tiltawhirl or teach me to tie my laces.

My mother worked as the manager of Kovacs' Drycleaning, and I was allowed to go with her and play while she manned the shop and ran the presser. I played hide-and-seek with myself among the racks of pressed suits, smoothed my cheeks against the skirts of rayon dresses. When I was tired I climbed onto the shelf below the cash register and curled up with my blanket. From there I could see my mother lift the presser arm, adjust the shirt, bring the arm precisely down. Again and again she repeated this series of movements, absolutely perfectly timed. Her graceful precision pleased me immensely, and I lay on the shelf watching her until heat and drowsiness overwhelmed me and I fell asleep.

Kovacs didn't mind me being there because Mama was industrious. He had probably never before had anyone quite so good at running his business. Because he was making money, my presence could be overlooked. He would come in to check on things, and invariably things were buzzing. Water surged in tubs, masses of wet clothes churned in vats of starch, irons, and spot-remover hoses hissed, the presser clanked and belched steam. It was my mother who made these things happen. He puffed on thick cigars and was satisfied.

Life, I thought, was busy, productive. We were workers, the world was a place where people made things, did things. And it was this making and doing that made the world go. When my mother pressed shirts, swept linoleum, washed windows or brushed her hair, she seemed substantial, someone to be reckoned with. She made clothes clean, windows bright, and floors smooth. Produce flourished in her wake, flowers spread across earth beds. As we walked home from Kovacs' in the early evening she made pickups roll by, and a tractor at the edge of town pull a harrow through black ground. I heard far off the hiss of milk against the sides of pails, the soft thud of hens' eggs settling into nests. Because of her the grain elevator filled, we would have bread. The smell of bread rising, the sound of the treadle sewing machine, these were her talismans.

What I wanted was to be where she was. Where she was the current was faster, the light more brilliant, the colors brighter. Air turned stale when she was gone, scintillant when she was there. She enhanced the ordinary present with her presence, made the quotidian more interesting than otherwise. I felt not that something was about to happen, but that something was happening now. I learned the reverberations of moment heaped upon moment. A word was important because she had spoken it, the vibrations of her voice continued to energize the local air indefinitely. A chunk of granite flecked with mica became a sacred stone because she picked it up, put it down. When she left a room, the space kept a faint residue of her presence. Nothing alive and touched by her hand could ever again be simply dull, dead matter.

She left dishes undone to help me perfect handstands, wrestling and giggling with me, tumbling me against her. She was lavish with hugs, making a big to-do lifting me to her lap, urging me closer, settling me against her. She read stories, taught me cat's cradle and witch's broom, laughed prettily at my remarks. She talked the butcher into giving her sheets of butcher paper for my drawings. And she got down on the floor on her hands and knees and admired the accumulating crayon, urging me on to grander sweeps all the way across that great, open field.

When I looked at pictures of families in magazines, it didn't occur to me to imagine myself grown, with a husband and child of my own. These pictures referred only to us, now: I was the child, she was the mother, this was a fact that would not change. I expected to spend my life with her, and at the very least I wanted her to notice me, recognize the intensity of my passion. I blazed with fidelity. For the opportunity to perform some act of service I could endure inconvenience, discomfort, insult. I rushed to open screen doors, car doors, church doors for her. I brought her hourly offerings—nosegays, the best weeds, rocks, and feathers. I would bring her necklace from the dressing table, borrow cups of sugar, mail letters in any weather. I even went out alone in the dark to roll up the windows of the Chevy.

I was a kind of miniature, inept attendant, an awkward, dwarf lady-in-waiting. I'd go anywhere at all, wait any length of time. I waited with snow melting inside my galoshes, my mittens wet and beginning to freeze. I waited with an empty stomach, a dry mouth, a full bladder. In heat or cold, waiting to pay the water bill, standing on the sidewalk amid the din of gossip, I nestled against her haunch, clung to her dress or the sleeve of her muskrat jacket. And when I couldn't stand up any longer, I sat down cross-legged on floor or sidewalk and looked up at her.

Sometimes I hoped she would be a little sick so I could bring her boxes of Kleenex, aspirin, cups of soup. But if there were no errands, no arduous tasks, no extra gratification I could bring to her, then waiting was itself a busy activity, using up calories, leaving me worn out but with a sense of accomplishment. I was the kind of slave every despot dreams of, moral judgment suspended, burning to do service.

When I began to get the idea that she wanted more than we had, that she hoped to escape Kovacs' for something bigger, I was disappointed. I had thought it was work itself, that marvelous motion, that was the point. It had looked that way to me when I looked at her: *let me be in motion like her*. And if I came to her whining I had nothing to do, my mother was indignant. "The world is filled with things to do," she would say. "Build cities, tame rivers. Take out the trash."

But for my mother Kovacs' wasn't paradise. This marvelous enterprise was something dimmer, less divine than I'd thought. She had begun to talk about cities, to incant the names of distant places. San Diego, Los Angeles, Monterrey. San Francisco, Portland, Seattle. When she said these names her eyes looked away from mine, looked above me into the distance. She threw herself into work at Kovacs' like she was throwing something noxious away.

The more dissatisfied she became, the harder she worked. We started going to Kovacs' earlier, staying later. When I watched her now, hurrying, a drop of perspiration at her temple, I saw this motion beginning to wear her away, grain by grain. It was as though at Kovacs' she was locked in combat with some force she had to best.

"Hurry," she said. "You have to take a bath, quick." She stood beneath the door's arch, her shoulders vulnerable, nightgown just touching the floor. "Hurry, please." Behind her the early light, dim gold. I heard the first bird, a dove.

I slid out of bed, followed her down the hall. While the tub filled she pulled the nightgown over her head, stood at the sink, and turned on both faucets. Her breasts hung soft and loose, the hair of her crotch tight curls, blond with a reddish tinge. She washed her face, her throat, her shoulders quickly, oblivious to light, the music of the water. Hurrying, she dried herself. Her mind raced ahead, to Kovacs', to business.

The hairless fold between my legs was dampsoft, I put my hand down there to feel my oils. I liked the smell, the taste on my fingers; I would undo the bodice between my thighs, like I pulled the laces from my shoes. The dove cooed softly. I began to hum. Then my mother turned to me. *Not now,* her look told me. *We're in a hurry. Some other time, not now.* And she lifted me into the tub, soaped a washcloth, scrubbed me hard, as though pressure were speed. Rinsed me fast, lifted me out. With a towel she smothered my nakedness, closed the million pores of my skin.

She left me then, walked briskly back to her bedroom. The light had lost its gold flush. The dove, silent. What I heard was water draining from the tub. A sad sound, water leaking slowly down a hole.

Still I adored her. Or I had determined to adore her, no matter what: I did not want paradise with qualifications. I wanted paradise pure. If it was not quite so, still I might pretend it was. August, the county fair, my mother's hand in mine. "Please," I said, "can we look at the pigs?"

We walked through dusk to the livestock barn, under the wide doorway draped with bunting. The roof vaulted over low pens, muddy aisles. A din of snores, cacophony of squeals. I had seen pigs, fed my grandparents' sow and piglets, but I'd failed to notice the phenomenon of pigs: so there was crudity on the graceful earth. Who, I wondered, was responsible for hog and sow, waddling fatsacks, coarse skin stuck with wiry hairs. Front, back, top, aslant, there is no angle that redeems swine. To God they're beautiful, I speculated, and screwed up my face, tried to imagine this God.

Amid muddy straw and squealing porkers, my mother stood in red pumps, lush crinolines radiating from her waist. Above the ruffles of her blouse she frowned at the nature of things: pigs were not to her liking. A spotted sow grunted, sniffing through the rails. Crudity for contrast, that must have been the reason, I decided. *This* God was more plausible, I could visualize him. He was educated, traveled, he loved beauty, and he had seen my mother. He had seen my mother bending to cultivate the base of lilies, walking down colonnades of wheat. *Too perfect,* he thought, it lacks complexity. Her alabaster countenance requires swine.

So he made pigs to set her off. I was happy with this explanation. She tugged at my sleeve, and we walked into starry dark, crossed to the produce building. Inside, I dawdled near Edith Bicrachek's embroidery. GOD BLESS THIS HOUSE. HE HELPS THOSE WHO HELP THEMSELVES. THE MEEK SHALL INHERIT THE EARTH. I leaned toward color, awed by fine stitchery. But my mother read the words and became incensed. She squeezed my hand too tightly. My mother knew which way the wind was blowing, and it was blowing out from the plains toward both coasts, picking up houses, factories, department stores, and drive-ins in its swirl and depositing this architecture at the edge of both oceans. In Seattle and Los Angeles men drove long silver cars; women wore furs and danced to jazz. Clark Gable was somewhere in one of those cities, and my father was even farther away. In 1947 the closest airport was in Chicago, nine hundred miles away. She had seen film clips of U.S. Air Force planes zooming for Tokyo, but she had never actually seen an airplane. She was still stranded mid-continent, the biggest news on the radio the market price of wheat.

Other mothers hoped to shield their daughters from wickedness: mine would save me from perfect baking, the bad influence of too much crochet. She whisked me past Mason jars of Minnesota Wonders, hurried me out under the expanse of stars. Her face was emblematic, a carved prow of a Nordic ship stranded on land. She looked both ways, as though expecting a stagecoach. She would invent some fabulous vehicle for our escape.

"We'll ride the Ferris wheel," she announced. I could feel her determination to rise above the toy shooting galleries, the plain and its flimsy people, this brief sprinkle of balloons. We walked toward the revolving lights. My grandmother and grandfather on the ground would dwindle, a little bride and groom on a cake, and my mother and I would find the coast, see Gable in the flesh, maybe even cross the ocean and find my father. I would go with her up and out, step beside her onto the radiant round. The pulsing hub would be our instrument. My mother and I would make it in the sky.

But would we?

I kept up this fantasy as long as I could. Then, after a while, I couldn't. Things were not so fine as they'd once been, and I had to acknowledge that this might be a message. Maybe progress was a pretense, maybe life was really a downward slipping.

But there ought to be one thing, I reasoned, just one thing each person could keep high up. In a motel in Nebraska I made my move. We were going to visit my cousins in Omaha, and Kovacs', for the moment, was behind us. It was late in the autumn, most of the leaves had fallen. I slept that night with her in the double bed, and when I woke in the morning and went to pee, I noticed the key in the bathroom door. It was a crude skeleton key, the lock the kind you can pick easily. I took the key back to the bed and examined it, turning it over and over, noticing its curious metallic smell, wondering if my mother would let me take it home. She lay in bed yawning and stretching while I tried the key in both sides of the bathroom door and in the front door keyhole. Then she sat up, went into the bathroom, turned on the shower.

I peeked through the keyhole. There she was, soaping herself under falling water, singing. Through the flimsy curtain I saw spray glancing off her back. She was still beautiful; it wasn't too late. There she was, slippery and precious to me, there was the key in my hand. It occurred to me that I could have what I wanted. I'd say, "Don't worry, I'll be right back." Then I'd take money from her purse, go out and buy mashed potatoes and gravy, sweet pickles, angel food cake. The thought of this food was exciting. Pickles! We'd laugh, and I would eat as many pickles as I wanted. I began to fiddle with the key, it turned easily. Then I tried the knob. The door was locked, I'd actually done it! I could keep her now as she should be kept, lovely and safe from work.

But as soon as I realized the bolt was really sunk, a terrible knowledge came to me: my mother would not be happy in this bathroom. She would not want to spend the rest of her life there, I was suddenly certain of this. Soon, very soon, she would want to come out and get dressed. I panicked, berating myself, fumbling to undo what I had done. The key had turned easily, but now it would not turn back. I heard my mother turn off the shower, still singing. I sat down on the bed: at any moment she would try the door. The fact that my wish to keep her prisoner was ludicrous concerned me less at that moment than the fact that I could not perform the simple act of turning a key in a lock successfully. I sat, rigid, muscles constricting, shrinking with fear.

Still humming, she tried the door. "Honey?" she called.

"What," I said.

"Is the door locked?"

"Yes," I said. Both of us paused. Then my mother spoke.

"Well please unlock it, dear, I want to come out and get dressed."

I stood up, tried the key again. Again it would not turn. Though my fingers coaxed and twisted mightily, the key remained upright.

"I tried it before," I told her. "It won't."

"Well keep trying, honey," she said with elaborately casual patience. "You can do it." Her voice took on that quality of hoping to inspire the listener to confidence. This was a trick that had often worked with me before, but this time my mother's fear scared me.

If she was afraid I couldn't do it, how could I possibly succeed?

I tried. Then I willed myself to simply disappear. Incapable of unlocking a door, incapable of magical disappearance. I was ruined, every way.

At some point my mother opened the window and began calling for help. I sat down on the bed again. What if help didn't come? What if it did? I longed for my shame to be over. But a flower picked could not be put back on its stem. What's done is done, my grandmother said as spilled milk spread across the tablecloth. I understood the finality of that statement.

The motel owner heard my mother's cries. When he knocked I let him in. He was a short man, and this increased my sense of my own ineptness. Even a short, not very spectacular man could perform the simple act of unlocking a door. For him the key turned easily. He tried the handle and the door swung open, revealing my mother wrapped in a white towel.

My mother looked at me. I was obliged to return her gaze. In a glance she assured me she believed this unfortunate incident was an accident. In a glance I assured her it would never happen again. She summoned her dignity and thanked the man. He assured her she had put him to no trouble, that in fact it had been his pleasure. He turned then and walked out, closing the door of our cabin behind him.

My mother's shoulders were as beautiful as ever, revealing just how easily she could be ruined, by what a hairsbreadth I had missed harming her in some irreparable way. She came and put her arms around me, gave me a casual squeeze. "It's all right," she told me.

I have forgotten my cousins' faces, the feel of their beds, if it snowed. Back home my mother and I were different together. The snows were deep that year, and when I had to stay inside I tried to be careful. I did not march around bumping into things, leaving a trail of wreckage behind me. I tried to subdue my lust for pickles, and I certainly did not whine. I kept my voice mostly down, cultivating quiet. Quiet was my work now, like keeping my room neat before my mother told me to, or straightening the doilies on the backs of my grandmother's armchairs. I tried not to need much of anything beyond the bare necessities—food, clean clothes, a little conversation. I did not ask for ice cream or the privilege of staying up late. And I declined butcher paper, that extravagance I did not now deserve. I allowed myself only coloring books. And I stayed inside the lines.

One day when the snow had begun to melt and patches of brown grass were visible, my mother walked up to the table where I was coloring and put her hand on my shoulder. I was going methodically page by page through the book. Christmas was far in the past, but the picture before me was a poinsettia. It was that time between work and suppertime when there was still light but you knew that soon the light would go. "Have you noticed," she said, "that most of the snow is gone? Pretty soon those turtledoves will be looking for twigs, and the wasps will start building a nest." She walked to the kitchen and came back with a cylinder of butcher paper. Casually moving my coloring book aside, she unrolled it before me. "Let's color something big," she said.

I picked up a green crayon and made the ground. My mother began to draw a tree on her side, an elm leafing out, as the elms along the north side of our house would do, and I picked up purple and pink and orange and red and began to draw my mother. She was bigger than I'd every drawn her, in a very full skirt and many crinolines, wonderfully fluffy hair and blue, blue eyes. I drew myself, too, smaller. Then I gave both of us high heels and put corsages on our shoulders. My mother was finishing a row of tulips. When she was done I put in the sun.

After that I began to pick up. I tried out my voice again, tinkered with volume, tested the low and the high registers. My mother did not seem to mind. A little havoc seemed part of the natural order of things once again. More snow melted and the red tips of peony plants broke through the ground. Spring came on, and summer was coming. I began to allow my exuberance practically full play. I had my mother's good opinion, and I could not complain.

I had my mother's good opinion, but once in a while I felt the tug of sadness like the current of a slow but constant river. I had suffered my first great shame. After all, because of me she had had to stand naked, save for a narrow towel, before the eyes of a stranger.

❊

❊

Mother and Child

❊

❊

A day in May. Peonies beside the steps sweat and open, petal after petal unfolding from their copious centers. Wasps, zizzing in slow dance, cling to a papery cone under the eave. Heat mutes the slam of a screen door, the fading drone of a car. Heat rises in shimmering waves from the earth, and the sharp cries of boys playing softball in the schoolyard come as though from a great distance, exhausted runners arriving with the message, dropping at last to their knees. A dragonfly hangs above the hot funnel of a hollyhock blossom, maybe forever.

All grassy ease, this place, the heart of the country. Ice cream socials, the Lutheran church. Breadbasket of the Nation. The war is over; maybe there never was a war. It's 1948 and three years have passed since Hirohito forced his resisting generals to surrender to MacArthur. Truman is president, and America is postwar and back in business. Truman calls visitors to the White House his customers. Stalin is still adhering strictly and faithfully to this agreement to be content with Romania, Bulgaria, and to give the British a free hand in Greece. Oppenheimer is still respected and is lecturing at Harvard. Trucking, agriculture, the stock market, shops on Main Street—these things run smoothly, reliably, and not too fast. The pace is reassuring, there has to be peace for this kind of methodical production to go on. Wheat, corn, and oats get planted, harvested, sold. God is great and God is good, Mom still bakes apple pie, Dad goes to church to pray for rain. Nature is big here and tends to cancel the plausibility of all but the present. There are those who have been abroad, farm boys shipped out to Asia on destroyers, who have tasted Philippine beer and the small, fiery mouths of geishas. But most of them no longer believe it themselves. Did all that really happen? The boys have come home and home is best. *Hemme ere beste* in gold lettering on the china plate above the kitchen range. Now when a veteran looks in the mirror it's to check the smoothness of his shave, not his eyes' assessment of history.

Behind the window Ethel's round, yellow cake is rising. Benny Goodman blows sweetly on his clarinet, and liquid sun pours through the window above the sink, flashing on china, pouring through soap bubble prisms. On the sill a tiny cutglass swan holds the violets Carolyn picked for her mother this morning. Carolyn sits cross-legged on the linoleum, swirling water in her teapot. There's a hairline crack in the teapot's spout—Ethel's glued it, but Carolyn can still see the fine seam reminding her to be careful. And there are two cups left, cups the size of thimbles. Now Carolyn sets the teapot on the red toy table between two dolls.

"It's ready," she announces. "Come now while it's hot."

"I know it's very good tea, dear," Ethel says, "but Mama's very busy. She has to hurry."

"Please," Carolyn says. A word that may make a difference. Ethel looks down at her. There is urgency in her daughter's face. Clearly this is important tea.

"Get a chair, honey. Climb up and you can help me, and we'll have this tea while we're working."

It's not how Carolyn planned this tea party, but a tea party isn't any good without her mama. She pushes a chair across the linoleum, climbs up.

"Delicious," Ethel says, sipping the tea and humming along

with Benny Goodman. Even in a hurry, Carolyn thinks, her mama is pretty, arms flashing back and forth, hands bright fish in the frothy water. She counts again the violets she picked: seven. One more, one less would not be so pretty. One more, one less would not be right. She likes it that she got the number just right, and it is wonderful to be here beside her mama, almost as tall as her mama, doing what her mama does. The day seems a kind of splendor, the smallest things good—hearing a dog bark, someone down the street playing a piano.

"Ethel?" The screen door squeaks, it's Eddie's voice. Ethel's brother-in-law, Joe's kid brother, who's lived with them since Joe Senior died. Eddie comes up behind them, slings one arm around Ethel's waist, the other around his niece.

"How's it going, girls?" he asks, hearty, kissing each one on the cheek. Ethel smiles but doesn't break her stride.

"There's beer," she says. He squeezes her shoulder, goes to the Frigidaire. The sleeves of Eddie's white shirt are rolled above his elbows—that's how the men do it, that's how Joe looks when he comes home from a day at the slaughterhouse, a day behind the meat counter. Eddie isn't a butcher yet though. Instead, he's come from high school, that prison where he's doing time. Though it's only a matter of time, he thinks, before he walks through those double doors into the world of important work. He'll work like a man, get the privileges they get, feel the power they feel. Now he practices, drinking whiskey and smoking Camels. Calling Mr. Rasmussen, the superintendent, a sonofabitch, though not to his face. There are things in Eddie's way, obstacles like Mr. Rasmussen, but time, he thinks, is on his side. Soon he'll gun his Chevy west, swirl Rasmussen in dust. He will drive west; he has this planned. In the West there will be no one to tell him what to do. He doesn't know anybody out West, he'll do whatever he likes. He opens a bottle of beer, whistling, imitating the swagger of older men, men with serious business to conduct, getting it done, quitting at quitting time, then going out drinking, looking for women.

Tires on gravel, the sound of an engine. Eddie stops whistling.

The muscles of his face just perceptibly shift and regroup. A clearing in the forest where a twig snaps and every rabbit, every caterpillar, every petal holds still. Carolyn watches her mother, her mother holding still, too, making sure. Taking in the news. Then the sound of the motor cut. Eddie begins to whistle again.

Joe, past the peonies, up the steps. Through the screen door. A man in white. White shirt, white butcher's hat, white canvas apron, though the apron is streaked with grease and dried blood. In it, Ethel observes, he is stiff, as though the canvas won't give, as though he has to stand rigidly upright. General, sir, attennn*shun*.

"Howdy," Eddie says. And grins. A nervous grin. A cheeky grin. If he were in his Chevy now he would stop short, swirling Joe in dust. Give Joe the finger, get the upper hand. A cheeky grin, no doubt about it. Joe pauses, taking this in. Then he tosses the white hat onto the counter. It's been a long day at the slaughterhouse.

"I saw you," Joe says. Robert Mitchum John Wayne Kirk Douglas Alan Ladd.

"Yeah?" Eddie says. Casual, elaborately casual. "You saw me what."

"Don't play dumb, Eddie. You know what. All Main Street saw you, heard you, smelled the rubber."

Eddie grins. The old man is right on cue. It's true, Eddie did strip rubber, and it felt magnificent, and he wants to do it again.

"That was me all right," he says. Cheeky.

"And who's going to buy you tires, buddy," Joe retorts. "Don't think I'm going to buy you tires."

Eddie moans. "Christ," he says. "Rubber burns, metal burns, the sun burns in the sky. For Christsake have a beer. Hey Ethel," he says, his tone honing an edge of belligerence, "open a beer for your husband."

Ethel ignores this. Let them go for each other's throats, let them hack each other to pieces. Battle is not her province. She has round plates to wash and dry, she has a cake and a daughter to bring to perfection.

"Sure," Joe says, "let's have a beer, celebrate all that sweet black rubber laid down on Main, bought and paid for, but not by you."

"Jesus!" Eddie's eyes roll up like the movable eyes of a doll. "So it's Dad's money. So what. If the automobile had been around when Dad was seventeen he'd have done it too. He knew how to live. And he left us the money to live on."

"While we're alive," Eddie adds, as though there is some question whether he can count his brother among the living.

"Christ!" Joe says. Clearly this kid is hopeless, there is no point in trying to reason with him. He needs some sense bashed into his head, and bashing is the only way. A hopeless dope, cheeky beyond belief. Joe throws up his hands, heads for the livingroom. It's been a long day, maybe a man can find a little peace in his own livingroom.

But as he passes the little red table the toe of his boot catches one thin leg, table and teapot spray up, a cartoon explosion, pot and lid arcing through the air, then that sound: the finality of china shattering.

In the silence Benny Goodman's clarinet continues sweetly.

"Rats," Joe says, strides through the livingroom and out the front door, letting the screen slam behind him. Why are fragile things put in his way, things ought to be tougher than they are, more resistant to battering, battering is inevitable, he ought to be able to walk through his own house, he can't be responsible for every little china teapot.

Eddie shakes his head. Clearly the old man has lost it again, blundering through and leaving wreckage in his wake, no grace, no style. In some odd way Eddie feels he has won, at least for the moment. It's Joe who has made a fool of himself. Eddie takes another beer from the Frigidaire, goes into the backyard.

Ethel sighs. Carolyn is crying, and Ethel pulls the little girl to her, smooths her hair. The fineness of a child's hair is unanswerable. She strokes Carolyn's heaving shoulders. "We'll fix it," she says, glancing toward the oven. "Oh no," she whispers then, and

Carolyn, gathering back a great sob, turns in the direction her mother faces.

Together they watch the center of the cake collapse.

When Carolyn's sobbing had subsided Ethel let go, got the broom, and swept up the slivers, put them in a paper sack. They were done for, those bits of pieces; Ethel knew she could not fix the teapot again. Then she took the flattened cake from the oven and set it on the counter. She studied this ruin.

We'll have to let it cool and then see," she said. "Now I'm going to shell these peas. Do you want to help me?"

Carolyn nodded, dried her eyes with a fist. She was grateful for work, since she felt completely helpless to carry out any project of her own. The fact that she was actually able to stop crying was due only to her mama, she was sure, her mama's miraculous, calm persistence. Carolyn climbed onto the chair again and stood beside Ethel, picked up a pea pod. Eddie was okay as long as her daddy was gone. When they were together they fought, they became the thunder and danger of their voices. Sharp bursts of fire hurtling back and forth. And their bodies, the look of their arms, throats, and chests hardened into shields. Shots zinging mightily between them, and she and her mama on the periphery, shrinking back, staying quiet, keeping small, way back out of the way. At those times Carolyn held very still. She did not want them to notice her.

Eddie looked like her daddy and wore his shirt-sleeves the same way, wore the same kind of boots. These boots especially seemed to be everywhere and very big, very prominent. She kept her toes well back. When Eddie talked he sounded like her daddy, when they argued it was one voice arguing with itself, the volume increasing, crescendoing toward disaster. Though they were fascinating too: handsome, big men, striding around like God. Their suntanned arms gleaming in sunlight, their faces the faces of movie stars. She was attracted and she was repelled, she admired and feared them. But when they fought they *were* frightening, she tried to get out of their way.

Ethel stood beside her. They were quiet. They could see Joe outside, kneeling, sharpening the blades of the lawn mower with a file. Near him a robin, drugged with heat, pecked halfheartedly in the grass. Ethel tried to explain to Carolyn that her daddy had reasonable reasons for getting into fights and wrecking things. Daddies were men with responsibilities. Daddies had important work to do, and her daddy's work was killing cattle and you couldn't do that softly, and so he got out of the habit of being careful of china, cakes, and little girls. When he came home he was tired, and then Eddie would egg him on. Eddie looked grown-up, but he was still really a kid, and Daddy had to take care of him, they all had to take care of Eddie until he finally grew up. And then when you're mad you don't notice what you're doing and you accidentally kick things you didn't mean to kick.

In fact this was a speech Ethel felt compelled to deliver but did not completely hold with. She looked down at Carolyn's hands, small, chubby fingers beside her own, practicing deftness, trying to transform clumsiness into grace. There was the ruined cake on the counter. Ethel looked out at Joe with clear and visible impatience.

Benny Goodman came to the end of his riff then, and the announcer spoke. "Ladies and gentlemen, Harry S Truman, President of the United States." Harry began his speech. Ethel listened, not so much to the words as to the sound of Harry's voice. What a bully, she thought. The man's voice alone could make a cake fall. "We will not," Harry said, "I repeat, we will not compromise. We will not let our friends in Greece and Turkey down. We will show Joe Stalin and the Politboro that America is still the toughest country in the world today."

Ethel looked past the violets on the sill to Joe, his forearm like a piston again and again pushing the file along a blade. Sharpening a weapon. Men charged each other like mad bulls, Ethel thought, grown men still trying to prove themselves. It didn't matter where they were, what color their skin was. Her family had come from Denmark, Joe's father from Czechoslovakia, and it made no difference. They thought of life as a battle. Other men were the enemies, life was a contest, and pride insisted you fight. They would fight over the most casual remark as though the reputation of a whole country hung in the balance, as though they thought themselves as important as nations. The war wasn't over at all, it simply continued, as though men had to have it to do, as though they couldn't stop. Eddie, she knew, was in the backyard getting drunk in the grass. Joe would mow the lawn and after dinner the two of them would go down to the pool hall. There they would get into a fight with each other, get drunk, come home with their arms around each other's shoulders, leaning into each other for support.

There were times, Ethel reflected, when Eddie and Joe so exasperated her that she would have liked to shake them good. Yes, and then push them in opposite directions far, far apart. Like you separated children and kept them apart until they'd come to their senses. But, she reminded herself, even if she could carry out this fantasy, they would not come to their senses. Once she let go, they'd simply rush together again. Like magnets they couldn't refuse each other's challenges.

The pity was that everyone around them had to suffer, too, there was no way to ignore them when they went at it. You had to be there and try to stay out of the way. But sometimes you couldn't get out of the way. *You were there.* And it went on, Ethel felt sure, just about everywhere. There were surely, at this very moment, cakes falling in Russian kitchens too.

She looked down at Carolyn's hair. The light shone through strands of blond, as through a prism. And what had begun to rise in Ethel, angry now, began to melt, turn liquid, expand, and rise again. Not the hard block anger was, but a dense, airy sphere. Determination of a kind, but soft, resilient. It gave her definite pleasure to feel this billowing of energy in herself. This good substance was hers and she had plenty of it, she embodied it, it rose in her, propelling her. It was hers, it would not go away. Though Harry's voice drilled away at it, though the scrape of the file wore at it. It wasn't metal, what Ethel had, she couldn't be damaged like metal could be damaged.

Now here before her was this child, flattened, sunk down, quivering. Well she would find a way to fill this child again with lightness, infuse her with airiness, plump her up, blow on her gently like you blew on a hurt bird to encourage it to fly. She would do this: this was what kept things going. This was what you did, what you kept doing, repeating, until it took, until it would stay. Until Carolyn could do it for herself. Let them ram their heads together, let them go at each other, let them battle each other to the death. She had real work to do. She picked up a knife then, ran it around the circular edge of the pan, turned out the thin, leaden cake.

"Honey," she said as she began to wash the pan, "I want you to help me. We're going to make another cake."

Fallout

"FORTRESS AMERICA, that's what Taft calls it," my father told Voneda. Voneda tapped one of the Camels out of his pack, struck a match on his thumbnail. Voneda and my father were buddies in the Masonic lodge. What they did in this club was secret, even Mama and Betty Voneda didn't get to know. They wore rings on their middle fingers to show they belonged.

It was summer of my eleventh year. We lived at the edge of town where the fields began. From the windowseat I could see heat rising in waves from the plowed furrows. Outside the open window there were yellow jackets plying the mud beneath a dripping spigot. Also a pair of turtledoves had nested in our cedar tree. I spent a lot of time that summer watching their arrivals and departures, listening to their soft, bubbling coo.

"Come over here," my father said. His ring flashed as he turned the pages of the atlas. He wanted me to look. Education. Education was very important. "Taft says it's this long rectangle, South Pole up to the Japs, over to Alaska and across to Churchill, down Europe and Africa back to the pole." He traced this border for me with his finger.

"Right," Voneda nodded.

"Then Taft says we dig in. Hold the line all around the edge."

"Yes sir," Voneda said, exhaling. The smoke of this Camel was something to be reckoned with. "Don't let 'em get too close in the first place. Then when they start coming at you, you got time to get your guns out."

"Where are *we*?" I asked.

"Right here honey," my father said, pointing. "Right here in the middle. You understand this, sweetheart?"

"It's to keep somebody out?"

"Right," Voneda said. "The Commies. The Commies and their fluoridation."

"That's the stuff in our milk?"

"Nope," Voneda said. "You're thinkin' of radiation. Fluoridation, that's in the water. It's radiation gets in the milk."

"Fallout, honey, he means fallout."

"Yep," Voneda said. "That's why the Nesbitts are making that cement thing."

The Nesbitts lived a few houses away, Ed Nesbitt was the postmaster. He was a brother in the lodge, too, and Edna Nesbitt sang in the choir at church. Marlene was in my class. They had dug a great hole in their backyard, ruining the grass. The cement truck was coming that afternoon.

My father walked in long strides to the fireplace, then turned to face us.

"This country's the greatest country in the world and it's going to stay that way."

"Yessir!" Voneda said, slamming his fist down on my mother's Danish modern coffee table.

"Fortress America," my father said proudly. "Nobody's going to get us with their fallout."

"No sir!" Voneda said. My father seemed reassured and heartened by Voneda's support. His mood turned philosophical.

"Taft is a smart man for a Republican," he said.

"Darn right," Voneda responded. He ground out his stub in the ashtray and stood up. "Well," he said, "got to get back to the wife."

"See you at the lodge," my father said. They would meet after dark, do secret things with their rings.

"Yes sir!" Voneda replied. And he whacked my father on the back.

Outside in the alley there were hollyhocks blooming; you turned the blossoms upsidedown to make dancing girls. You could also float them on sycamore leaves, each leaf a gondola carrying many dainty dancing girls across the goldfish pond for a night of revelry. I imagined Fortress America as a castle surrounded by a moat. The dancing girls might go there to a ball, dance with knights, drink from crystal goblets.

Fallout, I'd got the idea, was a fine white powder. Like arsenic but smaller grains. Dandruff. Death's bad breath. I imagined my grandmother's chickens amid grain she had scattered for them, pecking placidly. A find white spray settles on their white feathers. They lift their heads and look around stupidly. Their heads turn oddly and too slow. Then one by one, making no sound at all, pairs of yellow legs fold. They are fluffy heaps.

And on the dark red backs of the Hereford and her new calf death would look like frost. The calf stops bawling, topples over. Her mouth falls open and her little tongue hangs out to one side. The cow takes longer. Slowly, heavily, she lies down beside the calf as though to protect it. Then her neck and head relax and she, too, gives in to limpness.

All this happened without a sound. Fallout made things shut up, fast. At the hollyhocks' ball the dancers suddenly stop. It has begun to snow, the finest flakes. The dancers look up. Slowly the horror dawns on them. Partners topple into each other's arms, collapse on the dance floor.

"What's fallout look like?" I'd asked my mother.

"There isn't any here, honey," she'd said. "Don't worry. Just run outside and play now. Have a good time."

I didn't believe her. Did she think I was stupid, did she think I could have a good time with this stuff flying around in the air? I imagined an invisible layer of fallout on the ground. Would it eat holes in my feet? Would it eat up the sound of my footsteps? Should I stop going barefoot? Would my hair fall out soon? Should we keep the windows shut at night, would fallout eat holes in our voices while we slept? Would I wake up in the morning mute?

I put on my Buster Brown shoes and went down the alley to the Nesbitts. Ed Nesbitt squatted, grunting and banging with a hammer, putting the finishing touches on the plywood forms. He'd taken the afternoon off from the post office, where he sorted mail, his ring flashing, his hands fat grubs gobbling the envelopes. Squatting made his breathing noisy. Maybe he had been swift once, but it was clear he would never move fast again.

I crouched down behind the cedar bushes. Marlene came out then, letting the screen door slam. Her belly, like his, sagged over the elastic band of her shorts.

"Let me help," she whined, jerking the corner of his collar.

"Stop that," he snapped.

"Give me a turn," she whined again. Ed went right on hammering. "Daddy," she burst out, "you're not letting me!"

"Marlene," he snarled, "you just get back inside with your ma!"

She burst into tears then, went stumbling toward the house. I was not sorry to see her crying. I did not see how she could stand to be such a fat pig. And I hated the sound of her voice, a whine that would drive God himself crazy. If she had been my girl I would have spanked her and made her change that voice. I played with her sometimes, but only when I was desperately lonely and could not find anyone else.

I heard then the sound of the truck. It came like a tank advancing down the alley between the hollyhocks, two rows of colonnades. The driver backed into the Nesbitts' yard, and I shrunk down beside the bushes and held my ears against the roar. The truck knocked down several hollyhock stalks and kept going all the way to the pit. Then the driver tipped the mixer and the cylinder opened and began to pour.

I stood up then, scared but determined to see. The earth seemed good to me the way it was. When my mother turned it over with a trowel it fluffed up light and lay there looking rich and prosperous. I had a spade of my own and a personal garden plot where I grew beets, green beans, and daisies. You could tell the ground liked being handled and turned, and I worked there a little every day of summer, loosening the soil, feeling the lightness of the heft of each spadeful, the lift that was part of the earth itself. Fat worms drilled their passageways easily through it, my mother said their tunnels gave the roots of plants an airing. When my grandfather plowed his fields the plow cut excitingly deep. You walked the furrows and sunk down slow and softly. It was a material far superior to sand, which felt, when you walked through it, lifeless, dry. You could tell by walking barefoot through a freshly plowed field just how good the corn would taste.

Edna and Marlene appeared behind the screen door's mesh. Edna was a skinny woman and her face was always bright red. I despised her absolutely. The combination of skinny mother and fat daughter struck me as a terrible misfortune and an absolutely perfect match. They did not open the screen door; they were staying well out of the way. Sweating and shouting at the driver, Ed flailed the air with a shovel, trying to push the wet mass where he wanted it to go.

When my father made the goldfish pond, he'd mixed cement quietly by hand. He had let me put my handprint in the bottom, and I knew it was still there, my small mark, pristine among the roots of water lilies, the flitting fish. But this cement was different. The noise was huge. This was serious, political cement, and it was going to be final. It meant to make the ground shut up, to keep out air and sun, the buzzing of yellow jackets, the coo of doves. No fish would bask serenely here, no lily pads shimmer in sunlight.

Then it was done. The driver climbed into the cab, drove back down the alley and away. Many pink skirts lay in the dirt, their flounces crushed. Cement was a bad answer, I thought, to the problem of fallout. Any fool could tell ground shouldn't be beaten and smashed down and covered up. Ed moved from squat to squat, smoothing the surface of the wet mass with a trowel. He looked small beside the mass of wet grayness, and the scrape of his trowel was tinny, a paltry thing. The Nesbitts were going crazy, and they would surely have to pay for their sins.

People were pretty much like ground, I thought. If you tried to live in a cement bunker you'd die from being pushed down and shut up. What you had to do with fallout, I decided, was fight it in the open air. In the open air you had the helpful power of the earth under your feet. I vowed I'd keep my eye on things, look for signs. If we saw evidence of fallout coming, we could stand our ground. We'd let them know we simply wouldn't stand for any ruination.

"Ed," Edna yelled, pushing the screen door open, "you come in to supper now."

"Uh," he grunted.

Then she saw me. "What you doin' here honey?" She stood in the doorway, narrow as a stick, picking her nose. Marlene stared at me. I decided I would not give them the satisfaction of an answer. I stared my hatred of their cement right into Marlene's eyes and refused to look away. "You go on home before dark," Edna said, threatened, it seemed, by my hostile presence. "Ed says you go on home now."

Ed of course paid no attention to her and said nothing. Sweating, he stood up, wiped the trowel on his pants leg. Then he lumbered to the steps, heaving himself up step by step, and went inside.

I walked boldly up to the cement, felt the damp surface with my finger. It was already setting up, I could feel it hardening. Already my finger left no print.

It was a Cadillac of cellars. I'd got Marlene to show me—she wasn't supposed to play there but she wanted to impress me. The Nesbitts had paneled the walls with knotty pine, and above the fireplace where fake logs sputtered hung the head of an elk. Ed, I supposed, had shot it when he was young and agile. Two leather recliners faced the elk, and Edna had folded a plaid hunting blanket over the arm of the one that was Ed's. On the floor lay the hide of a huge grizzly, its claws reaching for the four corners. It lay very flat, as though hit, crushed by some weight falling straight from above.

The shelter had an iron door, thick layers of iron fastened together with bolts and rivets. On the wall just inside the door a chart, two columns of numbers. I examined this chart. Between the columns stood a woman wearing a tailored suit, a white blouse, and khaki tam. Her right hand pointed toward one column, her left toward the other. She was blond with terrific teeth, Doris Day as a WAC. The numbers on the left, Marlene explained, indicated amounts of fallout. The numbers on the right told you how many days to stay inside the shelter for the corresponding amount of fallout.

I shifted from foot to foot, wishing I'd stayed in my room. There were windows in my room, big ones looking west. From them you could see where town stopped and countryside began. You could see heat rising in waves from the fields, and a tractor, tiny in the distance, turning over a dark, wet furrow.

Beneath the chart, leaning against the wall, a pick and shovel.

"What are those for?" I asked.

"For digging out, stupid," Marlene said. "For digging out after the blast."

It was dark. Soft summer dark stretching for miles, the dark of the universe. Fireflies, a breeze in the elms. A dog barking sounded holy. Voneda and my father had gone to the lodge meeting; lodge meetings now were held in the Nesbitts' shelter. Mama was washing dishes. Across town Betty Voneda was probably washing dishes too. I supposed even Edna Nesbitt was washing dishes. They were all of them drugged, I thought, with the doing of so many dishes. I intended never to have to do dishes if I could help it.

"Will it be real loud? The blast I mean."

"What blast?" my mother asked, scraping a pan with steel wool.

"The bomb." She looked at me.

"You mean the atom bomb," she said. I nodded. She took off her rubber gloves then and turned to face me. My father, she thought, was responsible for this, she imagined he'd been educating me again. "Listen," she said, "there isn't going to be any blast."

"How do you know?"

"Take my word for it." They stayed the way they were, those women. Through anything. They could take it without batting an eye. They would hang out clothes while lightning struck to the right and left of them. They would peel potatoes while the waters rose.

"What about the Nesbitts' thing?" I persisted.

"Honey," she said, "listen now, I'm going to tell you what's what. There was a blast once, but that was a long time ago and it was far away. By now all the fallout is gone and it never came near here anyway. That place of the Nesbitts is just a clubhouse. They drink beer and play cards and talk." And she put on her rubber gloves again and began to scour another pan.

One morning I found the mother turtledove stiff at the base of the tree. It was late July. Sprinklers whirred. Roasting ears were ready to eat. I climbed the tree. The nest was empty. I had seen the baby birds practicing. Now with no mother they had flown away.

I'd been keeping an eye on things, and there were signs that things weren't so good. On the leaves of the elms I'd detected a fine white film. And sometimes there were tiny specks in the mud beneath the spigot, as though someone had spilled powdered sugar. I'd asked my father about these specks.

"Flaking paint," he'd said, looking up at the side of the house.

My mother was on him to get some painting done, but he hadn't yet.

I didn't believe him. Evidence kept coming in. I picked up the body of the mother dove and carried it inside. My mother and father were arguing about a box of instant mashed potatoes. My mother lusted after new things—frozen orange juice, Frank Sinatra records, net, and chiffon. She had recently bought a Mixmaster without asking my father.

"Jesus Christ," he'd said, "another gadget." He saved old things. My mother's blond Danish modern coffee table stacked up with rubber bands, matchbooks, paper clips, Dagwood and Blondie comic strips cut from the newspaper which he intended someday to paste in a scrapbook.

"The war is over," she'd say. "We do *not* have to save rubber bands."

In the basement he kept his grandmother's fainting couch, cloudy mirrors, chairs with broken legs, lengths of frayed rope, buckets of bent nails. His voice would rise from the cool dimness of the basement.

"Ethel! What have you done with my copper wire?"

"What would I do with copper wire?" she would answer matter-of-factly.

Now my father held up the box of potato flakes. "We don't need this," he hissed. I held out the dead bird.

"Look," I said. "Fallout."

"Oh for heaven sake," my mother said. Then she addressed my father. "You see what your education does." He let this pass. It was early in the morning and a long, hot day in July stretched before him. "It probably just died," my mother continued, addressing me. "These things happen sometimes."

I looked at her with contempt. I knew about turtledoves. Under normal conditions they lived a long and happy life. And we were in the middle of a perfectly good July.

"They don't just die!" I said.

"Don't you worry now, sweetheart," my father said, patting my shoulder. Then he went out the back door and started his panel truck. My mother put the box of potatoes away and began to clear the breakfast dishes. Voneda, I imagined, was smoking a Camel while Betty turned his eggs over easy. And Marlene, I thought, was probably stuffing herself this very minute. While I held this cold bird in my hand Marlene was biting into a sticky bun, not caring one whit.

Everyone was calm as cream. I looked down at the bird in my hand. My throat felt suddenly stiff. It occurred to me then that it might be happening already. Maybe I was already going mute, the inside of my mouth gray, hardening. Maybe they were all calm because it was happening to them, too, slow and quiet. They'd be dead before they knew it. My father would slump down over the wheel of his truck, my mother would topple over, her hands still soapy from the dishwater.

I rushed upstairs to the bathroom and ran a glass of water fast, gulped it down. Then I opened my mouth to the mirror: there was my tulip-red tongue, the veins under my tongue still blue like they should be, and in the back of my throat my little tongue, faithfully pink, a tiny dancing girl.

"Ahhhhhhhhh," I said. It worked, my voice worked. I stood at the mirror, growling. Barking. Meowing. I repeated the Lord's Prayer, then the Pledge of Allegiance. Then I sang out the national anthem, belting it out about the rockets' red glare, the bombs bursting in air, proof through the night that our flag was still THERE! Then I collapsed on the floor, laughing—though at first I didn't recognize this laugh as mine: it was a foreign sound, this laugh, like a bundle of barbed wire unrolling. Crawling on my elbows and knees like soldiers in the movies, I kept up this scratchy laughing, rolling and dragging myself down the hall, through the door of my bedroom. I rolled over and fell onto my back: there above me were the pink wallpaper blossoms of my ceiling.

I lay there, looking up at these dainty frills of flowers.

"Can I have that pot to play with?" My mother was phasing out the cast iron, phasing in the copper-bottom stainless steel. She gave me the iron pot. She'd already given me her dated black crepe dress, and I went up to my room and put it on. Then I took the pot out to the alley where the hollyhocks grew, tied three sticks together and suspended the pot from this tripod. Into the pot I put a handful of bottlecaps, a bunch of bent tin-can lids, some rusty nails, a bar of soap, crushed leaves from the elm trees, a feather fallen from the turtledove's wing. I added a couple of cups of dirt for binder. Then I carried water from the goldfish pond and stirred the mix with a stick.

While this poison cooked, I danced around the pot, chanting. *Earth, sun, earth, sun.* The ground and the sun were two things that worked together. Ground took sun into it and made plants grow, and plants grew up, offering themselves back to sun. My black dress began to absorb sunlight, heating me, making my power strong. I became a black mass of heat, hot enough to ripen roasting ears, hot enough to melt cement. All right, I would take over this alley, I would chant and make it safe for democracy. If I danced hard enough, fallout would not dare come down.

Marlene came shuffling down the alley then to see what I was doing.

"What's in there?" she asked, leaning close to the pot. There was powdered sugar on the end of her nose.

"Magic," I said. "I'm doing my magic."

"What can you do?"

"Just about anything," I said, rising to the occasion.

"Make me thin then," she whined. "I want to be popular." She had a summer cold and her nose was running. Apparently she had forgotten about my glaring daggers of hatred. Apparently she trusted me completely. Like her father, I decided, she was stupid. "Mary Jo did it," she continued. "She has a double chin but the rest of her is thin."

I nodded. Marlene was right about Mary Jo's physique and social status.

"Well, can you do it?" She said this like a challenge.

"I can make your fat invisible," I said. "But you'll never make cheerleader. I can do magic but I can't work miracles."

"Just try!" she countered. And she took a deep breath, sucking all the snot back in.

I considered.

"Okay," I said, "I'll do the spell for you. But you can't cry. And you can't say anything until I tell you you can talk again. Now, get down on your knees and say *please help me.*" She looked at me, pleading. I was lead. So she got down, her knees on the sharp stones of the gravel.

"Help me."

"Say *please.*"

"Please!"

"Here we go," I said. And I dipped my hand into the pot. "Your cheeks are too fat," I said, smearing goo on both sides of her face, "we'll have to get rid of that." Then I smeared goo on the folds of her neck, and on her arms and hands and fingers. "Stand up," I said, and I rubbed goo on her feet and legs. I spattered goo up and down across the back of her dress and over the rolls of her belly. She stood there like she'd promised. Muddy and desolate. I noted this with satisfaction. Then I took up the stirring stick and began my chant. "Fat, fat, fat, fat," I chanted. I danced around her in time to my chanting and each time I said *fat* I whacked her one lightly with the stick.

Fat face, fat cheeks, fat neck, fat neck,
Fat arm, fat leg, fat pig, fat pig.

I sang this over and over, I danced and whacked and chanted. She stood absolutely still. There were tears in her eyes, but she did not make a sound. And I ignored her tears. I told myself I could not stop for any reason at all. I drove myself on into this frenzy, I beat myself against the fact of fat. Like a whip I cracked myself against her. I rode this crest of myself the way wind rides all the way across a cornfield, rippling the leaves and tassels. There was no stopping me, I had unleashed myself. And I kept it up, chanting and dancing, until I was sweating, until I had built up my nerve to its highest pitch.

Then I stopped, stood in front of her, and spat out the final couplet.

Fat legs, fat legs, fat feet, fat feet,
Get out stupid fat pig, here's some fat for you to eat!

And I shoved the stick between her teeth.

I let her stand there, tears coming down her cheeks, her shoulders slumped. She was still completely silent. When I thought a sufficient time had elapsed, I yanked the stick out of her mouth and flung it down. "Go home and wash it off," I said. "You might feel it but nobody can see it."

She turned away. As she stumbled off she began to sob little wisps of sobbings. They were shocking, these cries of hers, each one a faltering, ranging all up and down the scale, each one a weak leaking away, a quavering warble. I stood there stunned: I had had no idea that beneath the brute dullness of that fat these sounds were inside her, sounds more delicate than yellow jackets' most fragile mud combs.

I saw the dove then. I'd laid it down beside the hollyhocks, intending to give it a proper burial later. I began to feel a little sick. *You know something?* I said to myself. My mother often said this when she was about to deliver a bit of information she considered vital. *You're dumber than I thought.* I thought of my mother washing dishes, of my father tending his customers, chatting with them about Fortress America, and of the Nesbitts going down into their hole, locking that iron door behind them. *You and Marlene both are doomed to set the table*, I continued, *while the poison comes drifting down. And don't think you'll escape the dishes either.*

I told myself I'd go see how the yellow jackets were doing now. I'd ask my mother if we could have roasting ears for lunch. I'd put on my pink sundress and assemble a group of dancing girls and take them on a picnic. I thought of these things to do, but I stood very still. I stood very still, and a single hollyhock blossom fell from its stalk and landed at my feet. It fell onto those sharp stones, and lay there on its side, still.

Snegurochka

Wilson, 1944. A town with a depot. One train at noon is all the town's sound. A town so small it needs only one barber, my father's uncle Joe. My father and his buddies cruise the Pacific, binoculars sweeping the horizon for enemies who want America dead, and Mama and I live with Joe and Mary in rooms, sunny, above the barbershop. Wide rooms, spacious, turned to face the sun, wood floors sun-warmed for my bare feet. Mama helping Mary bake bread, smell of yeast rising to the flat above. At night Joe drinks beer in the kitchen and plays the accordion. The squeeze box puffing sound toward me, wheezy music billowing up, floating the floor of my room. An accordion singing in summer dark, and Mama and Mary bending and lifting as though winnowing grain, lifting a soft white sheet above their heads, letting it drift down, nimbus, settle over me.

Nothing is missing. My father isn't missing, he waits handsome in a gilded frame on top of the piano, waits for General Marshall to discharge him. Every morning I go downstairs in my nightgown, slide onto the piano bench, salute him, and improvise military music. While sun spreads across the carpet I play reveille and taps and Sousa marches. Where I am is where everything is:

spreading sun, one train's steam and whistle, and Mama and Mary, one for each side of me. Mama sleeps with me, Mary makes the noodles. I have all I need.

I have all I need and a kind man too. My uncle Joe smiles down at me from busy tallness, snipping his way toward dusk with silver scissors. Every day the town's strong men wait in line to give up their strength to him. Willingly they sit sacrificial in his chair, black leather on a marble pedestal, willingly they lay back their heads, exposing the tender jugular to his razor. *Nolo contendere* they mumble in Russian through lather. *Not too short* they plead.

My uncle taught them kindly. It was the same lesson over and over again. He bared the weak flesh of their cheeks, and when he'd finished and held the mirror for them, they understood all too well how they'd hidden the truth from themselves. *You're not so handsome as a year ago*, the mirror said dryly, *so live you fool: to be alive at all is lucky*. Afterward the sun hurt their eyes. They walked home with heads lowered and did not kick dogs. Strangers and women could see the white napes of their necks. Their new humility seemed precious, they swore to themselves they'd never forget again. That night they had to be fed soup, had to be helped to bed by women.

The next day they could stand alone, eat meat in the evening. My uncle had given them easy wisdom, but they were mortals and soon forgot. Daily their hair and beards grew back, daily they became more careless. As the month progressed they refused their children nickels, kissed their wives less frequently, turned their backs in bed. Their biceps hardened, and they could stack more bales longer. But strength was dangerous—like yeast batter it had to be used when it was ready. If they tried to store it, their bodies might puff up into monster shapes a woman's little finger could puncture. To use up strength they whipped the milk cows home with switches, curdling the cream, drove their tractors late and too fast. One gunned his tractor through the wall of the barn, ruining a whole flock of white chickens. Nights they spilled whiskey on the seats of their pickups, rammed pool cues through windows. Past midnight those who still had too much power careened home and fell across their women in the dark.

Saturday mornings they woke worried, hurried down to the barbershop. Uncle Joe was happy to take their hairy power, and they were so relieved they gave him money too. He was the only man in our town strong enough to have pulled down the First Presbyterian Church if he'd wanted to. He could have been the star of a movie bigger than any of us, snapping rafters and joists, bending organ pipes, hurling down the iron bell to crack to pieces on the sidewalk. But he was so powerful he didn't need to prove it. He liked beer but never got drunk, and he gave free haircuts to hobos who jumped the train near our town. On the shelf beside the shaving brushes he kept a jar of salt water taffy for children. And he drove the moaning wives of servicemen to the hospital in the next town to have their babies. He knew the difference between harmless play and real power, and Saturday after Saturday they came back to him in the nick of time, waited on benches like pews to be saved.

Like Sergei Petrovitch and Maria Nikolaivna, Joe made the money and Mary made the noodles. He left her to the peace of the eggs and the calm of white flour, she stayed out of the barbershop and darned his socks and underwear at night. He stacked up the coins and green bills and she starched the organdy curtains and boiled the plum dumplings on Sundays. The other six days of the week she rolled dough circles as thin as linen, draped these circles over the backs of kitchen chairs to dry. She let me feel the dough's smoothness, how the texture changed as they dried. She gave me bits of dough to eat, and at noon she fed us chicken noodle soup with celery salt.

"Mary," Joe would say, "these are damn good noodles." When they were alone they talked secret words, but when Mama or I ate with them they spoke English to be polite. "You make better noodles than my mother made, don't you ever let anyone tell you you don't make good noodles." When it was time to go back to the barbershop, he hugged my shoulders. "Have some more noodles," he whispered.

When company came his kindness didn't hide in the cellar. "Sit down Ed," he'd say, "don't be in such a goddamn hurry. Mary wants you to taste her noodles. You've got your whole life in front of you and not a damn thing to do in this town. Enjoy life a little, have some noodles."

Like Sergei Petrovitch and Maria Nikolaivna they had everything they wanted except one thing. In the afternoon when schoolchildren passed the barbershop on their way to the drugstore, Joe and Mary looked at each other and sighed. One January day Mary, wrapped in sweaters, shawls, and babushka like Maria, put down her shopping bundle on the back porch and began to roll a ball of snow. When Joe saw her he opened the window.

"Mary, what the hell are you doing?"

"Making Snegurochka," she replied. "You can help me if you want to."

So he pulled down the fur flaps of his hunting cap and came outside to please his good wife. And in no time at all they had made a little snow girl with a dear round head and white dress.

"If only she were real," Mary said, "I could give her a bowl of noodle soup."

It was at that precise moment that Mama and I came to live with them. I rushed ahead, held out my wet red mittens to them, laughed at the surprise on their good faces.

"Snegurochka!" my uncle Joe exclaimed. Aunt Mary looked into my eyes—they were wide blue open, and my gold hair blew in the wind. She had heard my silvery laugh. I spoke to prove I had become flesh.

"Have you got any noodle soup?" I said, hoping enough time had passed to take the rudeness out of asking.

Mama had to work all day, but I was unemployed and real. Like Sergei, Joe carved wooden dolls, made their wigs from real hair gathered from the floor around his barberchair. The snowgirl could eat only icicles dipped in honey or cups of snow sprinkled with sugar, and she had to sleep uncovered on a cool porch. But I needed Mary's goosedown comforters, and since I could eat more noodles than any other food, Mary got to go right on doing what she liked best in the world to do. Thanks to me she didn't have to be careful not to make too many noodles. Though I stayed thin, I didn't melt like the snowgirl, leaving Mary to weep over a puddle. All those noodles had made me substantial and the soup had warmed my blood. Mary was happy before I came. I just made her happiness bigger. She could tell me stories in the language she knew best, and though I didn't understand the words, I understood her voice, like strong linen thread, was sound she wove for me. I offered all the advantages of the snowgirl and none of the difficulties.

On Sundays Joe took Mama and me driving on dirt roads between cornfields and fenced pastureland.

"Aunt Mary, I wish you'd come along," Mama said. Mary smiled and put on her apron.

"Cars go too fast," she said. "I have bad dreams the night after."

Sometimes the wives of men waiting for haircuts came into the kitchen to gossip with her. She liked company but when they left she didn't pine. She was happy alone, pushing and molding dough, watching me sit in the garden dirt, tomato juice and seeds dripping down my bare front. Now when she talked to herself she laced thick words with chirps and trills, as though birds skimmed across the landscape of her vision. She had a secret other women didn't: rolling snowballs and dough circles was another way to make little girls. You only had to want a girl badly, to long a long time and buy fresh eggs.

Late afternoons, when my eyelids thickened and I couldn't close the screen door fast enough to keep out flies, when I couldn't eat another tomato and the peonies opening layer after layer out from their centers seemed too great a magnitude to bear, she sat in the rocker beside the west window and lifted me onto her lap. Graciously she let me lean into her, and I felt in the softness and contentment of her body a reverberating calm.

Mary's was the calm of fire in a cook stove. Bread would rise evenly and tea simmer. Her nerves were long strands webbing her to husband, to the kitchen place, to air, to garden earth. These strands didn't snap or buzz, but like wet leather stretched and retracted slowly. At night she wrapped these strands around her, and her wide body filled the close dark with fleshlight. Close to her I wasn't afraid of the dark. Not one afternoon of those years passed when she wasn't in that kitchen in her plenitude of flesh, lifting me when I was too tired to say please, when only my eyes asked for the smell of flour in her cotton dress and the mild, encompassing heat of her body. She was present always, the perennial soup in the cast iron pot, the magic pitcher never empty of cool milk, the bed that appears on the forest path when the heroine falls forward exhausted. Drowsily I burrowed into her, and in that rocker in sloping sun she held me on her lap however long it was until I woke. I thought she was the center of a circle so wide I'd never leave it no matter where I went, what I did.

But when I tried to grow up, I wanted to forget her, forget them both, and forget Russian, their language. I wanted to spit it out like I spit out chewing gum when I saw a boy I liked sauntering toward me. The blond girls in Coca-Cola ads had never heard those obscene peasant sounds I was sure, and I ached to be one of those girls, to wear white shorts, shave my legs, sip Coke, and refuse to have any past at all. When my father spoke Russian to me on the phone I thanked my luck my roommate couldn't hear him. And I pretended I couldn't understand.

"I should have taught you the language when you was a kid," he said, wistful through hundreds of miles of line. I hated hearing him say *the language*, as though that one was the real one, the useful one, the one worth knowing. It proved, I thought, how simple-minded he was. It was a clumsy language, I thought, and to speak it made men thickheaded and cruel, women forbearing and dull. But forgetting wasn't easy. It seemed not a day passed without remembering Mary rolling dough, her face serious as she concentrated on perfect circles, her eyes soft and wet as those of cows or deer. I tried to starve all of her noodles out of me. I was already slender, but I knew Russian girls turned lumpy and mute within the short space of a few years. Then American men didn't like them anymore. There was nothing for a fat Russian girl to do but go back to the old country. So I ate cottage cheese and celery and worked on increasing my vocabulary. If I shaved the hair from under my arms and got married so my last name would change, no one need ever know.

No one need know but me: I knew, I remembered. I never, never spoke Russian, but the words surfaced in my mind uninvited like old shoes rising to the surface and climbing back into the canoe. I remembered the worn linoleum in houses we'd lived in, the smell of cheap latex my mother used for what she called "brightening things up." And I failed utterly to deny my ancestors their favorite chairs.

So they were there, Joe and Mary, one sleeting night when another man pulled on his boots, saying he'd be back and I put my head on the table and sobbed. When I'd stopped crying I started thinking about Joe. Joe was the strongest man I'd ever known and he spoke perfect English and everyone in our town had respected him. I'd seen Paris, Delhi, Cairo, I changed the oil in the car myself, knew how to cheat on income tax, and I'd perfected a repertoire of ways guaranteed to get men to like me. I'd been proud of these things until now. Now I wondered how come a strong, good, handsome man like Joe loved Mary even though she was fat and never had learned English properly.

I decided I would stop trying to forget them. Instead, I would go and ask them. I thought surely they would still love me, they would tell me their secret. So I packed a suitcase and bought some presents—bath powder for Mary, a bottle of bourbon for Joe—and then I added oil and drove west.

When I walked through the front door of the barbershop in high heels and a tailored suit, carrying a patent leather purse of money and cards I could use to get more, Joe stopped his slow sweeping and frowned nearsightedly, waiting for the rich lady to state her business. I saw the red and white spirals on the barber pole, frozen. And through the window beyond my uncle the depot's paint flaked, peeling, and jimson weed grew on the tracks.

"It's me," I said, tinny keys to flimsy doors dangling from my bright red fingers. He came closer, trying to see my face, to make out words he hadn't clearly heard. Then I saw Mary. She stood in the doorway, yellow light from the dim kitchen behind her, a hunched figure with a cane, leaning forward and squinting, straining to see if the lady was someone she knew. Then her free hand fluttered, caught the doorjamb, and she propped herself against it, wedging herself with the cane.

"Aunt Mary," I said. She heard me but couldn't place my voice. Across the vast distance of that empty barbershop I measured her smallness. Even if I took off my shoes the top of her head would scarcely come to my breasts. "Who is it, Joe?" she asked, turning her body toward him, as when in doubt she had always done. I remembered that turning of her body, I remembered the pattern on the china and silver, the oilcloth tacked to the round tabletop, the red and white check organdy curtains, the hollow in the bottom step where our feet had worn away wood.

I remembered, and I alone remembered, and they whose help I most needed, these people from whom I'd taken ease, stored light and heat against the trials I'd have to face, these good people didn't recognize the slick, aluminum woman I'd become.

Slowly I walked toward them. "It's me, Snegurochka," I said softly. I hoped my voice wasn't too loud, too brassy, I hoped I hadn't startled them. I startled myself—I hadn't said my name aloud in years. It wasn't a cute name like Patty or Judy or beautiful like Donna or Dianne, and I felt myself begin to flush, saying it, it reminded me of plumpness, sweat stains under the arms, innocuous good will, and a low IQ.

Then I said it again, and there was a wildness in it this time, a sudden storm and thick, blowing snow, deep snow across all of Russia, across vast fertile land resting through Russian winter. Slowly and distinctly, for them and for myself, I repeated it, my real name.

"Snegurochka," I said, "I'm Snegurochka. Don't you remember me? The snowgirl, Snegurochka, remember?"

Bondage

I watch my mother slice an orange. It's 1946, and my father has been back from the war a few months. I am four. I have come downstairs in my blue nightgown, still sleepy, to look for my mother. My father has already left the house, and you can feel the heat beginning, heat that will overcome us with implacable force. I find my mother in a shaft of sunlight, slicing an orange for me to eat.

She did this every morning. An orange sliced: that intense color, wheels wet-bright on the plate beside my scrambled egg. Today she looks pained, anxious. Hurried. This mother of mine who was once serene, now since my father's return is beset. She moves through life as though she is on trial. This *seems* to have to do with my father's return, but I am not sure. It has occurred to me that I myself might be the cause, that I am a burden. I have become more conscious of my existence, how it—I—can be troublesome to other people. Is it my father? Me? Both of us?

I know two things about my mother. She is unhappy. And the other thing I know is my union with her. It's always there, our inevitable linkage. And then there is what we do about it: this orange she slices for me, this orange I am about to consume. Whatever may happen later in the day, there is the unchangeable fact of this orange, a thing of beauty, between us. The day begins with this magnificence between my mother and me.

My mother and I washed a lot of dishes together. 1950. Look at our backs, two women at a sink. Her pink crepe, dressy because it was Sunday. My white nylon blouse had puffed sleeves, my skirt a perfect circle of cotton, sweet-smelling. We had put up our hair. You can see the vulnerable napes of our necks.

She handed me a soapy plate. White circle, blue flower border. I rinsed it under the hot stream. My skirt spread roundness around me, ring after ring moving out from me. I was filled with an infinite number of circles, as when I dropped a stone in the pond behind my grandfather's barn, concentric rings spread across the water. Turning the plate under the water, I felt this spinning.

I asked questions. I asked the questions I could and did not ask those I could not. I could not say why are you unhappy? What is Daddy really like? Is there something the matter with *me*? Now while I scrape plates and scour pots, my daughter unloads the clean dishes from the dishwasher. Look at our backs, two women at a sink. Her rainbow shirt, my yellow turtleneck. Her Nikes, my sandals. It's the age of designer jeans: dresses are out. But we've put up our hair. You can see the vulnerable napes of our necks.

Now she asks the questions. Did it hurt when you had me? Did I cry a lot? Did Daddy take care of me sometimes? Do you miss him? Why are the kids at school so mean? Do I look funny? Am I a lot of bother to you?

My father was an accountant. Every morning he left the house at 7:30 and spent the day in the office of the company he worked for. My mother and I kept each other company. When he came home at evening he stayed pretty much on the periphery of the real action. The real action was whatever my mother was doing or said she had to do. Her work was not drudgery but making things go: potatoes had to be peeled, pillows plumped up, patterns laid out, and cloth cut and stitched. People had to be fluffed up like pillows. And above all everything must be beautiful: loaves of bread, floors, windows, gardens. She would not stand for ugliness around her. If my father wanted to read her something from the newspaper, she would listen briefly. But she tolerated his interruptions only so long. "Excuse me," she would say. "I have to make this cake now." Or she would stand directly in front of him and speak. "Please move. Can't you see you're standing where I'm mopping?"

My father was either at work or underfoot, as I was sometimes underfoot, sitting on the kitchen linoleum, playing as close to her as I could. He left the small box of his office and came home from work in a straight line, walked straight into her busy doing, which was circular and kept revolving. Her activity was a spiraling that did not stop. His straight line, when he came, broke into the swirling funneling she was. He could not catch onto her rhythm. He retreated to the livingroom and sat in an armchair.

Except on occasions when they collided. My father would complain he could not find something he needed. When he called up from the basement she had to take her hands out of the dishwater and go to the top of the stairs where she could hear him.

"Ethel," he said, "what have you done with my copper wire?"

"What would I do with copper wire?" she replied.

I knew what my mother was thinking. He was obstructing her progress as usual. She could not believe he had to take her away from the sink because some frippery like copper wire could not be found. She could not believe she had got into this situation where she had to put up with this man. He was bumbling and incompetent and forgetful and he came and put himself in her way, slowing down the life processes: window washing, childcare, the scrambling of eggs.

I took this snapshot just before we left for church. My father insisted we go to church on Sundays, and most of the rest of the world insisted on this too. God himself insisted on it, or so I believed, and so we went, leaving important work undone: the weeding of the garden, finishing the quilt for the Kuzaks' new baby. It's the early fifties, a Sunday in August. Maybe my mother had had a nightmare. Maybe a particularly nasty argument with my father. In any case she had decided that morning that God is rotten and stinks. She put on all the clothes she could find. Girdle, stockings and garters, brassiere, white slip, pink linen dress and matching jacket, shoes, earrings, wristwatch, pin on the jacket lapel. Her final act was to put on a hat with sequined veil, adjusting the veil to mute her eyes.

And gloves, white gloves.

I had seen her naked. I knew her breasts were really bigger, hung lower. No one could see through linen to her pink nipples, but I knew they were there. I knew she had a belly, lush, and a behind. And I was there watching when the minister and the congregation rose to sing "Rock of Ages." My mother rose with the rest of them, but her mouth stubbornly refused to sing. Through the opening prayer, the sermon, and the final benediction my mother set her eyes against God the way men set their jaws against the enemy.

I had been given a Brownie for my birthday, and I insisted on taking pictures whenever any of us got dressed up. The eyes, I thought then, squinting through the lens, the eyes are the most important part of the face.

Suddenly I see something I hadn't noticed. Her left eye is bigger than her right eye. Trained to look for symmetry, I had seen symmetry. Looking again, I see this isn't so. Her right eye, slightly wizened like a small apple, seems to be looking askance, off to the side. Perhaps it's this eye that keeps watch for my father. It is her left eye, her feeling eye, that looks straight out of the photograph, offering, welcoming, inviting me in.

I go to the mirror. As a child I cultivated a facial tick, a grimace in which I squeezed my left eye shut and forced the right open exaggeratedly far. I thought of this look as conspiratorial, an expression meant to say *You and I, we know the score.*

I was thirteen. Work hard, my father said, get good grades. And I did. Practice an hour a day, my teacher instructed, and I sat down at the piano and set the metronome going. Aim for first, my English teacher said, sending me off to the state spelling bee, and I did as she ordered. It was the age of the answer. You didn't question the questions. The questions I could ask became fewer and fewer. The ones I couldn't multiplied.

I practiced my grimace at the mirror. God knows what I hoped to achieve by such permanence. An acceptable modern face, I suppose. And I practiced so faithfully, the tick took. Now my face still seems vaguely off center. If you look closely, it is not my feeling eye that is large and frank. Instead, my public, cerebral eye addresses you straight on, gathering facts, computing, getting the right answer fast.

Today my daughter chatters. I have had the day off from work, a day in which there is plenty of time to get things done. I am polishing the furniture with lemon oil when she comes in, drops her books in a chair.

"Beth had the nerve to ask for my answers again! Sometimes I wish I didn't have the answers, but I do. She didn't ask nicely either. But I've had it with her. I said, Look them up yourself for once, it won't kill you. And in Health we talked about how it's hard to say no, you know what I mean?" I nod. "But Elena stood up and said *My friend and I don't have this problem. We say whatever we feel and the other one just understands.* I felt so proud to have her be my best friend! And Mom, guess what else: Raoul looked at me today! I looked up and there he was already looking at me, we looked at each other for about ten whole seconds!"

My daughter's eyes are both the same size.

I go through my daughter's album. There are a few photos of her father, and then he moves to another state, disappears from the album. The pages fill with photo after photo of me holding her, bending over her, looking down at her, shielding her with my arms. It is the constellation of mother and child, repeating like a litany, that fills these pages.

And here she is in her blue nightgown. No women in my family have ever worn pajamas. I still remember my own blue nightgown, the first one. When it wore thin and my legs grew out from under it, my mother and I looked for another just like it. Finally she made me a nightgown as much like the first one as she could. When it wore out, I got her to make me another.

When my daughter was three, I bought her a blue nightgown. When it wore out, we managed to find another almost like it.

What I remember is not the time spent with her father. I remember being alone and having a daughter. Though I'm on the go, busy, impatient, never in any sense of the word a madonna. Still, as I dress, drive off, park, work, stop at the store on the way home, wait in line, stop again at the pharmacy and once more to fill the car with gas, all the while I feel myself bending over her, shielding her, looking down at her hair, the top of her head.

At times I enjoy this. At times I hate the relentlessness of responsibilities. There is always something pulling at you. You've got to make money, you've got to pay the rent. You've got to sweep the floor and mop it, scrub up the splattered grease in front of the stove, scrape the dirt out of the corners. There are always corners and they are always collecting and filling with dust, lint, thumbtacks, spilled sugar, the flotsam and jetsam of our coming and going. I, too, want things beautiful, and there is always one more errand to do on the way home. Even when I'm at work I feel anxious. I telephone to make sure she got home from school. I telephone to say I'll be there in about an hour. And earlier in the day, all through the day I'm available, on call. At any moment I may have to leave work, rush to her. I work, but I'm ready to sprint at a moment's notice.

Tonight my daughter kneels on the floor, packing a suitcase. Tomorrow she will go to visit her father. A neat child, she makes the right amount of room for the toothbrush, she nests the shoes. Then she lays the blue nightgown on top to see if it fits. She will leave the suitcase open, wear the nightgown, and in the morning put it back in, close the lid. I have had a busy day—work, phone calls, hurrying to the grocery, making lists of things that have to be dealt with tomorrow. I feel a wreck.

"I washed your dirty clothes too," she says as I stretch out on her bed. "They're still on the line. And do you have a little bottle for some shampoo? And I need to take dental floss, can you buy yourself another one?" She pauses. "Is it hard having a kid?" she asks, looking up from her blue nightgown folded on top.

Sometimes I have bad dreams. In my dream last night my daughter and I stand at the front desk of a hotel. It's morning, and we are leaving. On the way out a group of men stop us. The desk clerk has stepped out and doesn't witness this. Forcibly they separate us, drag us off to adjacent rooms. Some of the men hold me down on the bed while the others take turns on me. Afterward I hear her in the next room, crying. Her voice a wail. I cover my ears, but I cannot not hear her, her voice that is no longer a voice. There is the possibility that I will go mad, hearing her ruined sound. "I don't care what you've done to me," I scream at these men, "I can take it, but you should not have let me hear my daughter cry."

I wake tense, go to her room, look at her. What a relief to see her sleeping peacefully—and yet there is no relief. I am still agitated, I will do something quickly. In the kitchen I take an orange from the basket, get a knife. I hurry. There is some reason, though I have forgotten what it is, why I must hurry. There it is, sliced, now slide it onto a plate. I stand holding the plate, and think *But she's still asleep*.

I sit down at the table. The house is quiet, the street quiet. The slices of orange almost unbearably beautiful. On the buffet in the diningroom I can see the photograph of my mother at fifty-two. A formal, studio photograph, my mother dressed up, chic in black, a rhinestone pin on her left shoulder.

In this photograph she is proud. She wears a look of happy triumph: she's made it. The pie is cooling, the laundry put away, and there is daylight left. She has accomplished all she intended. The vicissitudes of life have not ground her down. Instead, she rose and came to meet them, each one. Beauty has been brought forth for half a century.

Beauty has been brought forth for half a century, and something everyday—not my father, but something—gave her the oomph, propelled her into action.

Maybe the necessity of slicing an orange, then seeing, when the knife pulled away, that wet brightness: like seeing the inside of the sun.

I think I hear my daughter now.

About the Author

Marilyn Krysl has published several collections of poetry including *More Palamino Please*, *More Fuchsia*, *Saying Things*, and *Diana Lucifera*, and a collection of short stories called *Honey, You've Been Dealt a Winning Hand*. She received an NEA Fellowship in Creative Writing and her work has been included in the O. Henry Prize Stories. Her work has appeared in *The Nation*, *New Republic*, *Antaeus*, *Triquarterly*, and many others. She currently lives in Boulder, Colorado where she is the director of the writing program at the University of Colorado, and is working on a novel.